"Forget about Bernard. It's me you want tonight."

Revel's voice was thick as he trailed kisses over her neck and shoulders. "Tell me you want me."

Carla remembered what he'd said earlier about the Franck marriage, his admission that Vivienne was contributing to its possible breakdown. Perhaps Revel was actually trying to give Vivienne up and was using her as a substitute— still using her!

"Revel, please stop!" she cried.

His face was sheened with perspiration, and his eyes blazed with intense passion. Carla knew he was way beyond the grounds of self-control.

She pleaded in hoarse desperation. "Then please, at least believe the truth. Bernard has never been my lover."

He wrenched himself away from her and sat on the edge of the sofa. "You cold-blooded bitch! Even at a moment like this you can remember to lie."

Books by Jayne Bauling

HARLEQUIN PRESENTS

These books may be available at your local bookseller.

Don't miss any of our special offers. Write to us at the
following address for information on our newest releases.

Harlequin Reader Service
P.O. Box 52040, Phoenix, AZ 85072-2040
Canadian address: P.O. Box 2800, Postal Station A,
5170 Yonge St., Willowdale, Ont. M2N 6J3

JAYNE BAULING

rage to possess

Harlequin Books

TORONTO • NEW YORK • LONDON
AMSTERDAM • PARIS • SYDNEY • HAMBURG
STOCKHOLM • ATHENS • TOKYO • MILAN

Harlequin Presents first edition April 1985
ISBN 0-373-10775-7

Original hardcover edition published in 1984
by Mills & Boon Limited

Printed in U.S.A.

CHAPTER ONE

'Don't do this to me too often, please, Alistair,' Carla Duminy requested quietly as she dialled the number she wanted. 'Industry is my subject, not drought.'

The assignment to Zululand held little appeal. Born and raised in the desert, she had too intimate a knowledge of what drought could do, to the land, animals and people.

The editor of *Afrinews* studied her anxiously as she leaned against the desk he had vacated when she had asked to use one of his telephones. After all these years in the city, she was still as shy and secret as she must have been when she had first stepped out of the vast, arid desolation that was the Karoo, and he wondered if anyone really knew her. She was not classically beautiful, he reflected, with time to do so for once in his life, but with that sensational figure it had to be something of a miracle that she had been allowed to preserve that air of protection in itself. She seemed to create a space about herself that forbade intrusion, and her reserve was often mistaken for hauteur. He sighed, wishing he knew how she would take the additional piece of information he had yet to impart.

'Old Nash's orders,' he reminded her casually. 'He has great faith in you, Carla. He reckons you're brilliant. He raised the question of an exhibition when I spoke to him this afternoon.'

She looked up, carefully expressionless, trying to suppress the stifled feeling that assailed her whenever she felt she was being subjected to pressure. She didn't want an exhibition, but she supposed that in the end she would yield, as they all did when the elderly proprietor of the Courant Group made one of his suggestions which they all knew were really orders. She had seen the Old Man several times and had wondered at so quaint a little person wielding so much power. Conventional and pious, he always wore a suit, tie and hat, and could easily have been a comical figure, but no one ever laughed at him because his piety was equalled by his shrewdness. Even Alastair Carmichael feared him.

Bernard's telephone was buzzing, but he was being slow to answer. It was his private number at Franck Constructions, by which he could be contacted directly, and she let it keep on ringing, convinced he must still be there, late as it was.

She smiled at Alastair because he was looking guilty, and it still disconcerted her that she was important enough to merit such consideration.

'If Marigold is tied up with the opening of Parliament, which of the boys is covering the drought with me?'

'Hardly one of the boys.' Alastair was grinning rather uncomfortably, not at her but at the tall figure filling the doorway which led from his office to the large open-plan one where those under him had their desks. 'I was just about to break the news to her, Revel.'

Carla's knuckles turned white as her grip on the receiver tightened, but otherwise she was frozen into immobility as her wary eyes rested on the newcomer's hard, dark face and found confirmation of Alastair's implication.

'The bad news, by the look of her, Alastair.' The harshly taunting voice was a violation, and the slightly slanting blue-green eyes were habitually cynical. 'We'll use my car to get to the airport. I'll be waiting in the basement parking area. A black Lamborghini. Get down as soon as you've finished your call.'

She had no opportunity to reply. A voice crackled at the end of the line and, oddly breathless, she asked, 'Bernard?'

But for a moment longer, she stared at Revel Braden, seeing the cold scorn that made the strange eyes almost turquoise, and the derisive smile which was all he had ever granted her. Then he was turning and striding away, and she heard Alastair expel a sigh of relief.

'What is it, Carla?' Bernard's kindly voice prompted her, a voice that spoke in a language she understood, because he was from home, another child of the desert. 'You sound distressed?'

'It's all right.' He was probably her best friend, but she remained as private as he, and anyway, Alastair was listening. 'I'm just ... under pressure. I have to go to Zululand to take some photos of what the drought is doing. I'm booked on the last plane to Durban tonight and will probably be back late tomorrow night. Mrs Du Plessis is in hospital for a few days and I can't contact Marigold Vibor, so could you possibly feed Pasht for me tonight and tomorrow, and chat her up a bit? I've left the key under the geranium pot beside the door.'

'No problem,' Bernard assured her as readily as she had known he would. When you were hemmed in by the sophistication of glamorous city life and a demanding career, you welcomed a simple task like feeding a cat.

They talked briefly, mostly about Pasht, Carla's brown Burmese queen, but her mind was on Revel Braden and what she would say to Alastair in a minute. A tight anger was unfurling within her—pure anger. Fear would come later.

Alastair was looking cheerful when she rang off. He shook his head laughing. 'It's hard to visualise the giant among engineering tycoons finding time for something as prosaic as feeding a cat. That was Bernard Franck you were talking to? But you're old friends, aren't you?'

'Ever since you sent me to take photos of that bridge Franck Constructions did in the Boland. He was visiting the site and we talked and discovered we both came from Karoo farms.' Carla paused, looking at him, the almond shape of her hazel eyes touching her with an air of mystery. 'Revel Braden, Alastair? A drought in Zululand is a bit small for him, surely? Like, unimportant? He covers wars. I'm not stupid, you know. He doesn't even work for *Afrinews* apart from allowing us some copy when he's covering something in Africa. He's special foreign correspondent for *The Courant* itself and has several broacasting corporations around the world as additional clients. Did you think I didn't know?'

Alastair spread his hands helplessly. Her voice had remained cool and well-bred, but it had trembled faintly with the effort it cost her to sound so polite. Still waters, he thought, seeing the sparkle of resentment in her eyes. He ought to have known that beneath the quiet, watchful exterior was the temperament of the artist she was. She was too gifted to be as coldly passive as she appeared.

In a conciliatory tone, he ventured, 'Think, Carla! He has just got back from that hellhole in the Middle East. It's understandable if he wants to cover a situation where death is dealt out by nature instead of guns for a change.'

'But still death, always death for him. I don't like being manipulated,' Carla asserted, still in that courteous tone, for the belief that displays of temper were the height of bad manners was deeply ingrained in her. 'Remember that flare-up in Zimbabwe last year? Revel Braden wanted you to send me with him then, didn't he, but you refused.'

'I had Old Man Nash's backing then. He said it was no place for a woman, chauvinist that he is.' Alastair shrugged eloquently. 'A drought is different. He has approved this, Carla, and Braden is representing both *The Courant* and *Afrinews*. You know what the Old Man is like about keeping costs down.'

'But Revel Braden is behind it somewhere.'

Carla started gathering up her cameras from the two-seater couch just inside the door, and slipped the strap of an overnight bag containing a change of clothing over one shoulder, since her present outfit of pleated cream linen pants, a matching silky tube top with thin shoulder straps and short-sleeved blouson jacket would be impractical amid the red dust of stricken Zululand. She saw no need to reassure her boss. They both knew she was too professional to abandon the assignment when he wanted to feature the drought in the following week's issue of the magazine.

'So he fancies you, Carla,' Alastair suggested unwisely. 'So what?'

'But that's just it, he doesn't,' she denied on a faintly scathing note. 'Haven't you seen the way he looks at me? As if I were unfit to be a member of the human race. He has never even spoken to me. I've seen him here a couple of times and elsewhere on two occasions, and it has always been the same. He looks at me and smiles in that vile, cynical way, and that's all.'

'So why is he doing it?'

'God knows.' She shrugged gracefully, pausing at the door. 'From the way he looked—to punish me, torture me, teach me a lesson of some sort.'

'But why?'

'Perhaps he doesn't like my work.' She gave him a polite smile. 'I'll do my own developing tomorrow night and come in the next day, Alastair. All right?'

'Fine. See you. Take care.'

She walked through the outer office where some of the magazine's staff remained at their desks although there was nothing like the activity to be found in a newspaper office. She smiled shyly at those she knew, but her mind was on the trip to Zululand. Twenty-four hours in Revel Braden's company or the prospect of seeing what the drought was doing to the people

there—she didn't know which appalled her most, and
now that anger was receding, she felt the first flutterings
of fear within her.

Damn Alastair Carmichael and Nathaniel Nash for
doing this to her! Regardless of how Revel Braden
treated her, she would probably dream about the
drought for weeks to come. She sometimes wondered if
those lonely early years in the Karoo had made her
unduly sensitive or whether she simply lacked the extra
layer of skin that most other people seemed to have.
Either way, her vivid imagination made a coward of
her. With the self-knowledge so painfully acquired over
the years, she was aware that while she might be able to
bear personal suffering, she lacked the courage to
witness the suffering of others. Perhaps it was
cowardice rather than choice that had made her a
photographer of industry and its ramifications rather
than of humanity as an entity.

Between the *Afrinews* offices and the lifts was a
cloakroom, and Carla entered it, needing what little
reassurance her mirrored reflection could give her. At
least she was no longer the gauche child she had been,
but there was little comfort in that. She supposed she
was attractive enough in an understated way, with her
creamy skin emphasised by the natural deep flush of her
generous but delicately sculpted lips on which she
usually only wore colourless gloss, and the shape of her
eyes was unusual even if the colour was not, since hazel
was neutral, taking on the colour of her surroundings
and emotions. Her nose was straight and quite nice, and
her smooth, shining hair was brown and skilfully cut to
sweep across her brow and reveal the beautiful shape of
her head and the delicacy of small ears.

Her figure was something else again. Her only
boyfriend, an equine photographer who had eventually
emigrated to Australia, had described it as spectacular,
but it often made Carla uncomfortable. She could

accept her femininity, but was oppressed by the reactions occasionally evoked by an amazingly small waist, high firm breasts and hips that were slim but decidedly feminine in the sweeping line that curved into slender, shapely thighs. Men could be so—so blatant in the way they looked at her, and a few had needed more than her inherent reserve to deter them.

She knew she possessed a superficial sophistication, but she hadn't been born with it. She had crawled to it, a long, hard crawl, and in the end, wasn't it only an illusion, made out of a sleek hairstyle, the subtle use of make-up and knowing how to dress? The farm girl still existed, the reality behind the illusion. She was no longer shocked, and she never had judged, but she could still wince inwardly at some of the things Marigold Vibor said, and be perplexed by Bernard Franck's marriage because he and his wife seemed to lead entirely separate lives though they still shared that mansion in Bishopscourt.

A faint self-mocking smile lit her eyes as she turned away from the mirror. Alastair Carmichael couldn't have been thinking clearly when he had suggested that Revel Braden might be interested in her as a woman. The famous journalist's women were all ravishing and chosen from an élite, pleasure-loving stratum of society or else from the Visible People. Marigold had told her she had seen him dining with the lovely interior designer Noelle Malherbe last week on the night he had returned from the Middle East. Anyway, if a man liked a woman, he didn't, as he had done, invite her to help him cover a dangerous situation like the one in Zimbabwe last year.

But what was his interest, when the way he looked at her said he despised her? As the lift carried her down to the basement, Carla sought for clues, but there were none. She had never really met Revel Braden, never spoken to him. She had only seen him a few times, and initially he hadn't seemed to notice her at all. Then, a year ago, at the lunch party for a glossy booklet promoting Franck Constructions which Bernard had commissioned after seeing her *Afrinews* photos of his bridge, she had seen him and questioned Bernard about his presence.

'He's here in his private capacity,' Bernard had explained unnecessarily. 'That's my wife with him. They're old friends. They virtually grew up together.'

Carla had looked with mild interest at the journalist and the soignée blonde woman at the other side of the reception room and that was the first time Revel Braden had subjected her to one of those searingly scornful looks. The silent, sardonically smiling condemnation had been repeated a couple of times when he had happened to visit the *Afrinews* office at times when she was there, and then there had been that Sunday morning encounter when, once again, Bernard had been with her.

After a particularly heavy week in which his business commitments had included the necessity of attending several glittering evening affairs, Bernard had been desperate to get away.

'Just to do something ordinary for a few hours,' the Karoo farm boy had explained and the farm girl had understood.

He had fetched her in his car and they had driven out to Blouberg where they walked miles along the beach without talking, for they were both quiet people, and finally they had breakfasted at an old fisherman's cottage which had been converted into a popular café. It was there that they had seen Revel Braden, sitting solitary over a cup of coffee and wreathed in blue cigarette smoke. He had reminded Carla of a satyr, with those slanting blue-green eyes full of savage mockery as they rested on her carefully composed face. He had a debauched look that morning, his strong jaw darkly shadowed with a night's beard—his face almost as haggard as Bernard's, but while Bernard's fatigue roused her to sympathy, the other man merely looked excitingly decadent, provoking a disturbing sensation that filled her with resentment. He had left before they were finished, pausing beside their table to murmur an indifferent greeting to Bernard before briefly regarding Carla with one of those scathing smiles that were becoming painfully familiar.

A touchy pride had made her resentful, deeply offended at finding herself a focus of such derisive amusement. At first he had wondered if he saw beyond the successful photographer to the oversensitive core that made her vulnerable, but finally she had decided against this as an explanation. There was too much contempt, too much dislike in his attitude for so simple an answer.

There had to be some answer, though, and if she was to spend twenty-four hours in Revel Braden's company, she must surely discover it.

The prospect of those twenty-four hours hung over her like a portent of doom, oppressing her with a conviction of impending disaster. Damn him, and Alastair, and that little gnome Nathaniel Nash, and all the brotherhood of men who manipulated women for their own ends. Until this evening, she had looked upon her life as eminently satisfactory. At twenty-four, she was well known as a photographer of considerable ability, and those moments when she looked through a viewing lens were the most fulfilling she knew and the only times when she was fully confident. These days, there was no longer any need to accept the commercial projects which had caused her so much unease in the early years, although she had to admit they had paid for many things she cherished in her life, her car, the ground-floor flat in Gardens with its small paved courtyard and flight of stairs leading up to her studio, and, most important, better cameras and developing equipment. Now she was free to accept the few outside commissions that appealed to her and concentrate on the part-time lecturing she did at the university and her work for *Afrinews* which was issued weekly and had impressive circulation figures since it was read in most African countries, with a special French edition for the Ivory Coast, Mauritius and the Seychelles.

Her personal life was equally satisfactory, Carla considered, and Marigold was wrong when she kept insisting that she must be lonely and organising dinner parties with the purpose of introducing her to a series of charming, eligible but incompatible men. She had a few friends, enough for her needs. There was Bernard, and Mrs Du Plessis, the widowed neighbour who usually looked after Pasht when she was away, and Marigold who lived just a few blocks from her, and while Marigold might be unable to exist without her beaux, as she called the various men who shared her flat from time to time, Carla needed no company other than that of her beloved Pasht, sleek, svelte and seal-coloured, wise as only a cat could be.

She had been as happy with her quiet, ordered existence as it was given to human beings to be. She had been content, but now had come this shadow. Revel Braden. Renowned in some circles, notorious in others, he could name his price and receive it, with reason. He had been shot at, banned and imprisoned at different times and, at thirty-seven, showed no inclination to follow a safer way of life. Some said he had a death wish, others that the only god he worshipped was Truth. Certainly he had voluntarily placed himself in some highly dangerous situations in his pursuit of the truth, and there was a much-related story, fast becoming a legend, about how he had parachuted into an Arab state which had temporarily forbidden entry to the foreign press during a time of trouble.

It was also said that in addition to his Lamborghini, he owned a Honda, a machine of terrifying power which he took out whenever he returned from the carnage of war, on a wild, illicit ride, outstripping the wind and the daemons he had brought back with him, after which he would return to Cape Town and take one of his women out for the evening.

Revel Braden, reckless and pagan and wholly alien to Carla's calm, uncluttered life in which passion had no part.

He was waiting for her beside his elegant car, tall and lean in casual, close-fitting charcoal denims and a matching open-necked shirt. His mouth had a sensual cruelty as he smiled, glancing at his plain watch after flipping aside the military issue leather face-cover, and Carla felt the tension of slight hysteria within her.

'I wondered if you'd decided to back out.'

'You don't have the monopoly on professionalism,' she returned coolly, allowing him to stow her equipment in the car. 'But you're right, this isn't to my liking, at all!'

'I'm not sure it's to mine.'

'When you set it up?'

'One acts on impulse occasionally.'

'And regrets it? Oh, I hope you will, I do hope so,' Carla stated with gentle feeling, getting into the car.

'Certainly one of us will regret it,' he warned idly when he was seated beside her.

She knew he meant her. She said quickly, 'But how much of an impulse was it, really? None at all, it seems to me, when it was the logical follow-up to that time you tried to get me as your accompanying photographer during last year's Zimbabwean crisis.'

'You're right, of course,' he allowed blandly. 'But don't flatter yourself that it's something I've been obsessively planning during the interim. Simply, the opportunity presented itself and I took it.'

'Snatched it.' Cape Town on a summer night was magically beautiful, a gracious and graceful queen, but Carla hardly noticed as the car purred through the streets. 'I congratulate you. You evidently have Nathaniel Nash in your pocket.'

'Hardly that, but a degree of influence, yes. It pays to drop the occasional reminder of the offers I've had from rival newspaper groups.'

His arrogance took her breath, but it was justified, not conceit at all. His byline brought prestige to *The Courant*.

'Considerable influence, not just a degree,' she said quietly but caustically. 'Mr Nash knows I don't usually handle this sort of subject except to help out in an emergency.'

'Drought too real for you, too raw?' Suddenly Revel's voice was harsh, the smile he flashed at her brilliantly derogatory. 'You're afraid or indifferent, I'm not yet sure which, because it touches people . . . human beings, Carla. You don't deal with those, do you? You photograph effects, shapes against the light, gold pouring from a pan, dams and bridges and buildings. But drought isn't material, it's a condition.'

'I know drought,' she informed him, mildly scathing. 'I grew up in the Karoo.'

The Karoo, one of the world's greatest and oldest deserts, but for her it had been a living place, teeming with myriad life miraculously adapted to its environment. Lithops, the plants that were living stones, so difficult to see, and the other succulents, aloes, haworthia, euphorbia, mesembryanthemums, cactus; and too, cobras and the meerkatte which killed them, lizards, springbok, ostriches, giant spiders. . . . They had been the companions of her childhood, respected, feared or loved, and drought had been another almost constant companion which drew her father's eyes to the horizon several times a day while their dam dried up and they sowed wild oats in the cracks and the livestock got leaner.

The soles of her feet had grown hard, running over the baking veld in the freedom only childhood knows, but there had been no other hardening process and she had suffered for it. She had been born when her parents, as reserved as she, had been quite old and convinced that their son was the only family they were destined to have. In consequence, she had been indulged, though never spoilt, and despite the harshness of the terrain and the stark realities it presented daily, she had led a sheltered life, almost overprotected, since for the first dozen years of her life she had lived entirely on the remote farm, with special permission from the relevant authority to do her education by correspondence, so she had had little to do with people outside her family and the Blacks who lived and worked on the farm. At twelve, she had been sent, terrified, to a good boarding school for girls, also in a country district, so cities remained a frightening, exciting mystery to her. Crippled with shyness, she had pined like a small animal taken out of its natural environment, away from its own kind, but slowly and agonisingly she had come, over the years, to the knowledge that if she was to be independent and make something of her life so that its ending would leave a space, then her future must lie away from the farm. It would go to her older brother when her father retired and in consequence held nothing for her—nothing save a rarely found blend of freedom and safety. But by then she had been given her first camera and had some ideas about what she wanted to do, for the pride and ambition that made successful farmers of her father and brother burned as a quiet, steady flame within her as well.

She had come to Cape Town, to university, and it was her first knowledge of a city, of glass and concrete laid out in curiously heart-wrenching beauty at the foot of a great mountain. Conquering shyness, concealing vulnerability, she had come to love it, with its fascinating architecture both ancient and modern, especially in the winter when soft fine rain such as she had never known before fell for days and even weeks. Better still, she loved the first factories she saw, the first mills, the assembly plants, the sight of great industrial tanks or chimneys belching smoke. The alchemists the modern world called scientists or miners or engineers created magical special effects for her camera, great sparking arcs of fiery metal shooting upwards, liquid fire being poured, metal cold and darkly menacing or hot beyond the knowledge of living things. . . . She had flown over Lake Kariba, sweated in the bowels of the earth down mines in the Transvaal, Orange Free State and Zambia, and perched precariously on the scaffolding of a skyscraper in construction; she had captured the first opening of the sluice gates of a gigantic new dam and dangled dangerously from a half-built bridge in order to obtain an unusual angle.

It was her life, and here was this man implying that it was the wrong one, that she ought to be photographing the same sort of destruction that he reported on instead of the creative life-giving processes that went into building a nation's wealth.

He had not replied to her reference to her Karoo background and she glanced at him. He was concentrating on driving, but quite suddenly she felt overwhelmed by his nearness. His presence threatened her. He would be a man without mercy. Everything about him was hard, the planes and angles of his dark face, the slanting devil's eyes, the visible muscles of his shoulders and long, powerful thighs. Carla felt a sick, searing sensation in her stomach and quickly raised her eyes to his face once more, reluctant to define what ailed her. His mouth, now, was oddly—brutal, almost, sensual in its curve and lower lip, yet eloquent of a ruthlessness that appalled her. There was a savagery in him that was outside her limited experience of men and she knew she feared him..

She supposed it was the way he lived that had made him as he was. Going into the situations he did would have refined certain aspects of his nature, his judgment of a situation and its news value, for instance, and possibly also his reflexes, since he must often face personal danger. Too, facets such as strength of mind must have hardened into inviolability over the years, but surely there must have been a diminishing of such virtues as the capacity for compassion and outrage.

That was why he had that cruel, uncaring look, and why his smile was so devoid of warmth.

'Why?' she asked in her soft, courteous voice. 'That's what I want to know. Why are you doing this?'

'Don't you know?' He sounded idly amused. 'I've always thought you were slightly unreal, and this confirms it.'

'I don't understand you,' Carla murmured distantly.

'You don't understand people, period,' Revel taunted. 'The human race. How can you? You don't feel, so how can you comprehend what others feel?'

She felt far too much, if only he knew. She fully understood that he was deliberately insulting her, perhaps with the intention of provoking a display of the feeling he accused her of lacking, but despite the deep burning anger gathering within her, she remained too inhibited to express it.

'You haven't answered my question,' she reminded him impassively.

He laughed softly, a sound that terrified her. 'If you don't know the answer, I don't think I'll tell you—yet. You might decide you're not so professional after all. Ask me again when we're on the plane.'

'There's nothing to stop me backing out before we get on that plane,' she suggested rashly.

'I don't think you will, though. Whatever other womanly qualities you're lacking, I can't believe you were created without your fair share of feminine curiosity.'

'If I get on that plane to Durban, it will be out of loyalty to Alastair Carmichael,' Carla told him in a remote little voice. 'I'm not curious about anything you think, say or do.'

'You will be.'

She hated that threatening voice, and hated him. He was the sort of man she detested, harsh, aggressively masculine and without any semblance of consideration for her sensitivity. God, she wished there was some way of teaching him a lesson, punishing him for the way he was treating her, but she could think of nothing. She didn't even know what motivated him yet, and she supposed he was correct—despite her fear of him, she would get on that plane to Durban because she was curious. She didn't want to know why he seemed to literally hate her, but she did need to know.

Their flight was the last to Durban that night and half empty, so they were able to sit together, but until they had been served with drinks from the bar, there was no conversation between them.

Then, having decided that she could best protect herself from the inner disturbances he caused her by keeping their relationship on a professional level, Carla asked, 'How are we getting about Zululand tomorrow? Helicopter?'

'We'll hire a car,' Revel asserted curtly. 'I hate choppers. . . . The sound of all my wars, like ghastly theme music running through my life.'

He sounded wearily disenchanted and Carla knew he wasn't really talking to her. She glanced at him with mild interest but didn't make the mistake of asking why he did it if he hated it so much. She knew enough of men to be aware that many had a curious love–hate relationship with their careers, especially such careers as Revel pursued, sickened by all the job entailed but unable to give it up. A vocation. . . .

'Was that Bernard Franck you were calling from Alastair's office?' Revel's voice cut in on her musing, harshly critical.

'Yes.' She wasn't going to elaborate on any personal subject.

'Did you have to cancel a date?'

'No.'

'No, you don't go out much, do you? Mostly, he simply goes to your flat.'

Carla's eyes widened slightly. 'How did you know?'

'Vivienne told me.'

'Oh, yes, Bernard's wife.'

'Bernard's wife!' Revel mimicked savagely. 'You say it so calmly, and maybe it means nothing to you that he does have a wife. Well, why should it? Vivienne is mature enough to accept her husband's infidelity, however distressed she claims to be, but there happens to be a child to consider as well.'

'Justine,' Carla inserted automatically, stunned by the construction he had obviously put on her relationship with Bernard Franck. 'But——'

'He has discussed Justine with you, then?'

'Of course. He worries about her——'

'But he's too weak to give you up for her sake.' Revel's mouth curled without humour.

'He worries about her because she's fourteen and bored and unhappy,' Carla stated emphatically. 'Bernard and I are not having an affair, if that's what you think. We are friends, however.'

'You look so guilty when you lie that you should never attempt it,' Revel commented sardonically. 'Friends, as in platonic?'

'Yes!'

'There's no such thing as a platonic friendship

between men and women, as I'm sure you know. You can't make me believe that Bernard has never touched you, that he doesn't want you.'

'He doesn't.' Carla bit at her lower lip to still its trembling. How could such an error have grown up, out of what? She felt as if she were on trial, Revel Braden her merciless one-man jury intent on convicting her however much she protested her innocence, and too he was the pitiless judge who would sentence her.

'He'd have to be gay not to,' Revel bit out with one of those quick, brilliant but contemptuous smiles. 'Which he's not. How long has he been your lover?'

'He is not my lover,' Carla denied stonily.

'And all those late-night sessions Vivienne tells me you have at your flat? Don't tell me you just talk.'

'If Vivienne knows about it, it's because Bernard has told her, because he has nothing to hide. She must be neurotic if she thinks there's anything more—and yes, we do just talk.'

'About Justine, I suppose, and how he worries about her?' Revel wondered sarcastically.

'Sometimes,' she admitted icily. 'And do you know one of the reasons for his concern over his daughter? The fact that she sees too little of either parent. He has to work to keep her and her mother, so the responsibility becomes Vivienne's as she doesn't work, apart from a bit of modelling at charity extravaganzas. But she's never at home. That's why Bernard has to come to me when he wants someone to talk to, because even if he leaves his office as late as ten or eleven at night, Vivienne won't be home. If that marriage is in trouble, Vivienne is as much to blame as Bernard.'

'Don't tell me you fell for that old routine. His wife doesn't understand him, so he needs your shoulder to cry on,' Revel mocked cruelly.

'Bernard has never actually discussed his marriage with me,' Carla stated defensively. 'He never openly blames Vivienne for the state Justine is in. These are just things I've gathered for myself.'

'Because they're things you want to believe, to appease your conscience.' His look scorched her, making her experience a sense of shame she had no need to feel. 'It's probably a favourable sign that you do in fact have a conscience since it will make it that much easier for me to end your relationship with Bernard Franck.'

'And how will you do that?' she asked indifferently.

'By taking you away from him. Once you have known me as a lover, you won't want him anymore.'

With a cruel glint in his strange, fascinating eyes, he watched the colour drain away from Carla's face.

'But . . .' she snatched a breath, 'but you don't want me.'

There was something sinister in the way he inspected her, a hot, hard intention in his glance as it roamed over her high breasts and then lingered on her generously wide but still fastidious mouth.

'Oh, but I do, Carla,' he assured her on a drawling, amused note. 'I've wanted you for quite some time now, and I intend to have you.'

But he spoke so casually, as if he could take her or leave her, though having once decided to take her, he would allow nothing to stop him.

He had been right, Carla thought wildly. If she had guessed anything of this, she would never have set foot in this plane.

CHAPTER TWO

'AREN'T you finished yet?' Revel strode over to where Carla was fiddling with her cameras. 'What the hell are you trying to do—make it look pretty? Drought is ugly, Carla, it destroys, it kills. Don't distort it.'

'Don't teach me my job,' Carla advised in the frosty voice she had used all day.

'But it's not truly your job, is it?' he taunted as she fell into step beside him and they began to walk back towards the hired car. 'You don't deal in reality, you don't like it. I've watched you today, and seen how you reacted to those squalid villages, seeing the people crushed with despair, the bowed shoulders of hope-lessness in the queues at the emergency water tanks, the children with malnutrition and their sick mothers, the overworked medics, the starving goats. . . . And they all disgusted you.'

Carla's face was shuttered, betraying nothing, but even so, she averted it. She knew she would dream of all she had seen today for weeks to come, and wake weeping for a proud people whose losses in famous battles had never left them as defeated as sadistic nature did now. Most of all, the piteous, constant crying of the babies would haunt her. She had always loved babies. She felt oppressed by a sense of futility. There was so little she could do to ease so great a hurt, save take her photos and hope those with the power or wealth to do so would be sufficiently stirred to provide what relief they could.

Acutely conscious of the tall man striding easily beside her, she was aware of a surging resentment against the hostility that prevented him from seeing her clearly. Shyness had bred in her a deep reserve that made confession of her innermost feelings an impossibility, but even without her inhibitions, if she could have confided that it was not disgust but distress that she had experienced today, he would probably have refused to believe her explanation, just as he had her protest that she and Bernard Franck were not lovers. Last night she had been sceptical about his casual admission that he wanted her, but perhaps he really did. It would account for the way his unnecessarily harsh judgment of her was made from such an off-balance position. Despising her, he probably resented her and looked for flaws.

'Believe what you like, I don't care,' she murmured wearily at last, having stowed her cameras in the back of the car. She turned away to stand staring out over the desolate red landscape where only aloes and a few euphorbia survived.

They were in the middle of a great barren plain, cut by a stony, rutted road. On the horizon, a low ridge reared in jagged tooth shapes, but otherwise the cracked earth was flat save for vast gaping dongas. The erosion of the soil, by wind and animals, was pitiful, for what vegetation had once bound it had died under the drought or been devoured by starving goats. All who had once lived here had moved on to regions where the earth's torment was less total, and not even a single head of straying livestock was to be seen. It was a dead, abandoned land where others were merely dying, bleak and bereft in the early evening sun.

She thought of her father and brother and their deep, atavistic worship of the land, and of how this sight would sadden them. She remembered other droughts, in her own country, and the joy when the rains had finally come and blessed the desert with a fleeting season of riotous colour.

Her face wore a remote expression, the almond eyes

dreaming, and the man watching her was irrationally angered.

He caught her by the upper arm, swinging her round to face him. 'Don't turn away and ignore me like that, damn you,' he ground out with shocking violence.

Carla stared at him uncomprehendingly for a few seconds. Antagonism rose sharply in her, but it was blended with something else, an acidic excitement that caused her to tremble. His hard, lean fingers curving round her slender arm scorched her like a red hot clamp and the fierce glitter in his eyes was a shattering experience.

'I don't have to defend myself to you,' she said quietly at last.

'Or to anybody, because you don't give a damn, do you?' Revel accused savagely, his fingers tightening about the smooth flesh until she winced. 'That's how you can so easily set about breaking up Bernard and Vivienne Franck's marriage. My God, it's time someone taught you to suffer.'

'And you intend to be that someone,' she challenged bitterly, testing the strength of her arm against his grip.

'You had better believe it!' He laughed, a hard, reckless sound that rang with self-contempt. 'Though probably only the devil and his minions know why I want you as I do. Certainly the angels can't know. Usually I like my women warm and caring and generous. . . . How many men have dashed themselves to pieces against that ice-cold unconcern, Carla?'

'Revel, for pity's sake. . . .' It was the first time she had used his name. She was shrivelled by the blaze in eyes that had turned pure turquoise and she stared up at him.

The harshly masculine mouth twisted. 'Hell, despite that sexy siren shape, you're probably frigid as well!'

'Certainly, with you I would be. You. . . .' Unaccustomed to trading insults and possessed of a deep-rooted horror of hurting anyone's feelings, Carla hesitated. But he had hurt her, so she must continue. 'You disgust me. I loathe you. How can I not? You've manipulated me into this situation and proceeded to insult me, refusing to listen to me and give me the benefit of the doubt. I look at you and all I feel is revulsion.'

'I'll have to cure you of that.'

'Some fine day!'

'Do you think so?'

Revel was looking at her in a way that induced a curling sensation deep inside her. His dazzling glance skimmed her tense face and dropped to her body, its allure scarcely concealed by the perfect fit of the jeans and clinging low-necked black T-shirt into which she had changed at Durban's Louis Botha Airport.

'Please,' she murmured distastefully.

His smile held an alert, dangerous quality. 'Please what, Carla? Please make love to you?'

'Let me go,' she requested, attempting once more to tug her arm free of his vice-like grip.

'When I'm ready.' Now he held both her arms, dragging her roughly up against him so that her head fell back on her slender neck, and he looked down into her face with a burning mockery. 'By the time I've done with you, darling, you won't be cold and uncaring any more, nor will you be frigid. You won't be only half a woman, but whole—complete! And you won't address me in that cool, polite little voice again ... I want to hear you vibrant and husky with passion. I'll break you if I have to, to put that break in your voice.'

'How can you want someone you hate?' It was a cry of protest, wrung from her, and she shuddered against the hard length of his body, appalled by the bitter depth of his obsession.

'I've told you, it's a disease straight out of hell.' His voice was laden with self-disgust.

'Well, I don't want you,' Carla told him clearly.

'You will.'

One hand was moved to the back of her head, and his mouth descended to claim hers in a ruthless onslaught that made her rock and sway against him. Briefly she strove to be free, desperate with fright. She had never been kissed so degradingly, never had her mouth invaded in this devastating manner. It hurt, her lips were bruised and stinging, and the cruel fingers tightening in the thick silk of her hair made her whimper with pain. His other hand was at the small of her back, pressing her closer to him so that she was forced to acknowledge the hard masculinity at the vibrant, forceful centre of him which demanded her feminine surrender to his aggressive maleness.

Carla stopped struggling and grew very still, determined not to respond and hoping a little forlornly that he might be deterred by inanimate indifference. But something strange was happening to her. The pain in her mouth had become mingled with a wild pleasure, sharp and sweet, and she felt the lurch of desire in her loins. A stranger to passion, she had no idea of resisting, no thought of escape. Restraint fell away from her without any conscious decision to discard it and, sensing her growing response, Revel took merciless advantage of it, snatching her up to new heights of feeling and sweeping her irretrievably into the realm of the senses which, once known, could never be forgotten.

Pale lids dropped over her feverishly glazed eyes, her arms crept round his neck, fingers tangling convulsively in his dark, well-cut hair, and she stirred, trembling, against the hard, compelling urgency of his body. Revel's mouth left hers to move hotly over her cheeks to her eyelids and down again, his day-old beard grazing her smooth magnolia skin. His hands now moved about her body, sure and skilled and possessive, but without tenderness or regard. Her thighs, her buttocks, her hips, the sharp inward curve of her waist, her rapidly heaving ribcage and the thrust of her breasts were all subjected to passionate, contemptuous caresses which ignited a sparking, heated sensation that swept through all her being like wildfire until she felt as if she were being consumed by the fierce flames of the funeral pyre upon which she had already cast pride and self-respect.

Revel's lips left the hollow behind one ear to blaze sensuously along her fragile jaw and slender neck, pausing at the hot, satiny hollow at the base of her throat and then moving on to massage the taut upper swell of her breasts revealed by the low neckline of her top. Carla writhed erotically as she felt the rough caress of his tongue on her flesh and a harsh groan of unwilling pleasure escaped her.

He lifted his head, holding her a little away from him now and, instinctively, Carla's small hands slid inside his gaping shirt front, slender fingers curling into the dark springy hair that covered his chest, and he jerked spasmodically in response to her innocent, intuitive provocation.

His glittering eyes skimmed her face with satisfaction, noting the hot, helpless resentment in hazel eyes, the hectic spots of deep apricot colour burning on her cheeks and the crushed vulnerability of bright quivering lips. He was breathing as if he had run a race, so was she, and their skins were damp and sensitised, ultra-receptive to the slightest touch.

His voice was strangely thick as he said, 'I could take you right here and now in the red dust with a sky for our roof and the earth for our bed. It's a savage land and appropriate to the way you make me feel, but I've too much consideration for my own comfort. Now that I know I can make you want me, I can afford to wait.'

Carla jerked away from his hold and he made no effort to prevent her.

'You ... you're like an animal!' she accused
frenziedly, supporting her trembling limbs and body
against the side of the hired car, uncaring that the heat
it had absorbed from the sun was burning painfully
through her clothing. It was better than the depraved,
erotic heat Revel had created in her, and perhaps pain
was a fitting punishment for her wanton lack of control.

'It's what you've reduced me to, sweetheart,' he
countered bleakly.

'I feel sorry for you,' she scorned bitterly, lifting a
shaking hand to smooth her shining brown hair. 'You
called me half a woman. Well, you're only half a man—
a real man isn't afraid to treat a woman with ... with
gentleness, tenderness! But you don't even know what
those mean.'

'I know,' Revel contradicted her cuttingly. 'Because
most of the women I choose are proper women, and
deserving of that sort of consideration. You're not.'

'Because of Bernard Franck?'

'Because of that kid of his.' The lips that had
plundered hers so expertly now twisted with contempt.
'My own parents' marriage came under the same sort of
pressure and finally cracked because of a selfish bitch
like you. I was younger than Justine, five, and if it
hadn't been for Vivienne's parents, I would never have
known what home life was like. So, I guess this is for
Viv's sake, as much as Justine's.'

Carla's always quick compassion was aroused, but
she suppressed it. He had used her too badly to deserve
anything of her. Nevertheless, she realised that his
character had been tempered in a cruel fire. That was
what enabled him to do the job he did. She could expect
no weakening in him, no softness.

She said sharply, 'And so, for yourself, and Vivienne,
and Justine, you intend to ... to take me and use me?
Or is it an act of revenge, with me as a substitute for the
woman who took your father away from your mother?

But what makes you think I'll let you, when you're not prepared to give me any sort of ... of courtship or tenderness or regard? I do have the right of choice, you know.'

'What makes me think?' he derided with a crack of laughter that made her wince. 'Simply the fact that even without the gentleness you say you require, you want me, you fool. You have just proved it quite effectively.'

'Fool is right,' she flared caustically, feeling the prick of tears behind her eyes. 'I was surprised, but I won't give you a chance like that again. So what are you going to do, Revel? Force me?'

'I doubt if that will be necessary,' he retorted with sardonic confidence that made her want to hit out at him.

'You ... bastard!'

'Maybe, but you want me.' He paused and seemed to be looking inward at some bitter truth, if the light in his eyes and the line of his mouth were anything to judge by. 'If not as much as I want you. I've looked at you for long enough, Carla. The looking is over. Now I want to touch, and possess. ... God! Exactly how many lovers have you had?'

'None,' she replied sweetly, a little surprised by the question.

'Why bother to lie?' Revel taunted. 'That courteous. well-bred image is only your public persona. ... The private woman is all passion, I'm glad to know.'

'You're a swine!' Carla condemned somewhat theatrically, jerking herself away from the side of the car and getting into the front passenger seat, her shapely head held high.

Revel was still laughing quietly when he came round to the driver's side.

'You don't like being found out, do you?' he mocked ironically as they drove off.

'Shut up!' Carla's colour was high as she uttered the words.

The truth was that she had surprised herself in several ways that day. The memory of the way she had responded in Revel's arms shocked her, and she felt deeply ashamed.

I hate him, she thought intensely.

He had drawn from her behaviour that was completely out of character. Not only had she responded to him quite scandalously; afterwards she had also said things to him she would never have believed herself capable of saying, answering back, challenging. Normally she had so little to say to anyone, but she had been so angry and humiliated that the words had just seemed to spill from her before even her brain had scrutinised them. Even this hating was out of character; she didn't think she had ever hated anyone before.

Consequently, she was feeling lost, out of touch with her own identity. She wondered if she had ever really known herself.

And Revel Braden was to blame. If only there was some way of teaching him a lesson, forcing him to apologise for his brutal treatment of her . . . Carla drew a quiet breath. That was it. She would get Bernard to explain their relationship to Revel. It occurred to her that Bernard, as inhibited as herself, would hate such an embarrassing task, but for once in her life, Carla was prepared to disregard a person's sensitivity. She had to protect herself, or let this man destroy her. Once Revel knew the truth, he would be forced to grovel, and that would be her revenge for his relentless persecution. She would accept his apology and he would have no option but to retire from the field. She would be safe again, calm and secure.

Yes, that was what she would do. She wouldn't bother with any further futile protestations of her innocence. Let him hear the truth from Bernard when they got back to Cape Town. After that, she could put him out of her mind.

It occurred to her, though, that tranquillity was gone for ever. How could she ever forget the conflagration that had flared between them today? It would haunt her——

'I've got all I need. You?' Revel interrupted her tortured thoughts.

It took her a moment to realise he was talking professionally. 'Yes, thank you.'

'Then we'll make for Durban. We could forget about our fight tonight and check into an hotel, if you like.' He was smiling faintly, as if he knew what her answer would be.

'You know I wouldn't …. like,' Carla retaliated pointedly.

'And of course, Alastair Carmichael will be wanting our material at the earliest possible moment.'

'Plus, I have other commitments in Cape Town.'

'Bernard Franck?' Revel's voice had hardened.

'Actually, I was thinking of the part-time lecturing I do at U.C.T.,' she corrected him coolly. 'I've a lecture tomorrow morning.'

He lifted an eyebrow. 'University of Cape Town? You surprise me. You're so quiet, generally, except when your equilibrium has been disturbed. I wouldn't have thought you could find enough to say to fill a lecture.'

'Oh, I'm riveting on my own subject,' Carla claimed flippantly.

'Of course, and you're the expert.' Oddly enough, he didn't sound patronising. 'But why focus your talent in the one particular direction? Was it a conscious decision, I wonder?'

'What's wrong? Do you think they're unfeminine, industry, engineering … machines and buildings?' she mocked gently. She hesitated, shrugging and fiddling with her seatbelt, afraid as always of saying too much and thereby revealing too much, perhaps only to be found flawed and wanting by a critical listener. 'Until I left school, all I knew was agriculture in a country where ultimately nature must always determine success or failure. I had never seen a mill or a mine, never witnessed gold-smelting or diamond-cutting. To my eyes they were beautiful and terrifying, creative processes.... There was excitement and symmetry, light and dark, effects that challenged my camera.'

'And of course, though the human element is there as in all things, it's merely subsidiary, so you're not required to care, to get involved,' Revel mentioned and it seemed to her that once again he was condemning her. 'You want to stay cool and self-contained and uncaring. You've opted out of the tenet that each of us is responsible for everyone and everything.'

'Whereas you grow rich on other people's misery, other people's wars,' she hit back. 'You're as bad as the arms dealers who supply weapons for causes they don't give a damn about, as long as they get paid.'

His glance was contemptuous. 'I do what I do because occasionally, I hope, what I describe wakes up one of the fat cats or one of the wilfully blind such as yourself, and makes them realise what's being done by human beings to other human beings on this woeful planet of ours—the only world we've got, damn it, and we're destroying it and the whole fabric of life in a multitude of ways, and will continue to do so for as long as people like you refuse to face up to their responsibilities. God, you're too selfish even to look at and admit your responsibility towards the Franck marriage, and that kid, Justine.'

'And I suppose you've never hurt anyone—any woman I mean—in all your life?' Carla challenged sarcastically.

'Not knowingly or deliberately, anyway.'

'Until me.'

'Until I saw you and wanted you,' Revel said brutally. 'And I'm going to take you away from Franck, and once he knows I've had you, he won't want you any longer.'

Carla made no reply, deliberately hunching a shoulder as she suppressed a little smile. He would find out. . . . She was looking forward to the moment when he was forced to realise the truth. She would make him crawl. She was not normally vindictive, but he deserved some punishment for his arrogant misjudgment of her.

The depth of his desire for her still surprised her, as did his admission of it. Most men, in the grip of such a compulsion, would dissemble, but Revel hadn't hesitated to let her know how badly he wanted her. With a little pang of humiliation, she acknowledged that it had to be her body, the proud lift of her breasts, the wasp-waist, the symbolic curve of hips cradling a flat stomach and flowing into slender thighs. It was degrading to be wanted for that alone, the rest of her despised. She was Carla Duminy, not merely a shape, but a woman as unique as every other member of the human race, with hopes and fears and thoughts that were hers alone, with faults and virtues to be forgiven and accepted.

It hurt with strange poignancy to know that all she could inspire in Revel Braden was lust and contempt. Her cheeks grew hot once more with her thoughts and she turned her face away for fear that he should glance at her, gazing through the window at the arid landscape and hoping that her moment of revenge might come soon.

Revel had little to say during the long drive to Durban, and Carla was grateful for his silence. It was late when they reached the airport and there was just time for her to head for the Ladies and change back into the cream outfit she had worn the previous evening while Revel went through the formalities of returning the hired car.

His uncommunicative mood continued on the short flight back to Cape Town, although he smiled with a quick charm he had never directed at her, at their pretty air hostesses. Observing the effect he had on them, Carla admitted to herself that most women would find him attractive. Personally, she found his aggressive brand of masculinity far too disturbing. How could one ever be comfortable with such a man? Excitement and pain were no substitutes for peace of mind, but she knew that many women still thrilled to the dominant male. For herself, though, she would rather be coaxed than commanded.

When they landed at Cape Town's D.F. Malan Airport, it appeared that Revel was expecting to give her a lift home once he had retrieved his car from the protected parking area.

'I'll order a taxi,' Carla said, and instantly his fingers curled round her slender wrist, silencing her because her mouth dried at the first instant of contact and her heart drummed in her breast, a frenzied tattoo of nervousness and anticipation.

'Oh, no, Carla, I haven't done with you yet. Did you think I had?' Revel taunted softly, his grasp tightening on her wrist. 'I'm taking you home.'

And then what? Her frantic mind led her down a dozen fanciful paths. How should she resist him, were he to decide to seduce her tonight, before she had had a chance to meditate on her hatred and harden it into something stronger than the depraved hunger that gripped her when he touched her? She needed time in which to contemplate her chaotic emotions and settle them into the order that would best serve to protect her.

'You live in Gardens, don't you?' Revel said when they were in the Lamborghini, the airport behind them.

'Who told you?'

'Vivienne,' he answered curtly.

Tense and still, Carla sat silent in her seat as they drove into the city. Fatigue oppressed her, weighting her eyelids, and it was a further irritant to her troubled spirit to observe that Revel didn't share her tiredness. Last night, they had started the drive to Zululand almost immediately after their arrival in Durban, and she had been glad of it since she had thus been able to obtain some unusual views of the parched land as it met the sun rising to torment it for another day. Subsequently, they had been on the move all day, driving from stricken village to village, stopping briefly to ask questions and take photos, and now Carla was weary, depressed by the irremediable tragedy she had witnessed and deeply perturbed by the situation into which Revel had forced her.

Thus, her heart leapt with relief when they finally turned into the narrow road in which the flat was situated and she recognised Bernard Franck's white BMW parked beside the pavement. He must have worked late again and only now be feeding Pasht. She wasn't sure if Revel also recognised the car. His dark face was hard but expressionless in the soft light of a street lamp, and a thoughtful little smile suddenly quirked her lips. If only she could find the savoir faire to direct what happened in the next few minutes, she might even be granted her revenge tonight.

'Thank you for the lift,' she said politely, testing him, when they had both emerged from the car and he was handing her her bag and photographic equipment.

'I'm coming in with you.'

She bowed her head in acceptance and led the way through the wrought-iron gate set in the high wall that gave privacy to her small paved courtyard. The lamp on the wall beside the front door was on, illuminating the wealth of plants growing in attractively placed terra cotta urns or tubs made from old wine barrels, and the curving stone bench situated where it might receive the beneficent shade of an ancient oak that grew on the pavement and spread its branches over the wall.

'Why are your lights on?'

That irresistible little smile appeared again, tugging at the corners of her mouth.

'Bernard is here,' she offered in a neutral tone.

She sensed the stiffening of Revel's body, close behind her, as she opened the unlocked door to reveal her tiny hallway with its tranquil colours and more plants in fascinating containers, including a hanging basket of gracefully trailing ivy. From where they stood, it was possible to see through the open door that led to the lounge.

Bernard Franck sat sprawled, with closed eyes, in a low, comfortable armchair covered in palest peach corduroy, with Pasht draped in her favourite position over one arm of the chair, topaz eyes narrowed to slits, her seal coat gleaming, all svelte feline loveliness and far too dignified to acknowledge the fickle mistress who had deserted her for over twenty-four hours. Carla smiled involuntarily. With the vanity of her kind, Pasht always chose that chair, whether empty or occupied, for she seemed to realise it flattered her exotic colouring, and the covering fabric was somewhat marred by regular onslaughts from her claws when her pleasure at having nothing to do in life but look beautiful and lazily accept the homage she commanded became so intense that she was moved to kneading.

Bernard's eyes flickered open as he sensed their presence, and suddenly Carla was herself again, constrained by her own inhibitions and her naturally sensitive regard for other people's feelings. He looked so tired, and how could she embarrass him by marching in and demanding that he explain to Revel that he was not her lover?

As she stood hesitating, her earlier fancies dispersed

by the reality of the situation, Revel swung her roughly away from the door, removing both of them from Bernard's line of vision.

'A charming, domestic scene,' he grated in a low voice, turning her to face him. 'All right, you've still got tonight. You look tired, Carla, but you're not too tired, I trust, when the poor faithful fool has waited up for you. Give him a night to remember and then tell him goodbye. I don't want you to see him again.'

His hands were violent on her shoulders, but the effect of his touch was inevitable, and she swayed, her head bent as if in defeated acknowledgment of his power over her. Those long, steely fingers reduced her to a mindless cipher, destitute of all will—and it was wrong, and unnatural, when she hated him.

'You may think you can force a place for yourself in my life, Revel, but it will never be freely given. Is the invader ever truly welcome, and what rights does he have save those of might?' She moved her head in a negative gesture, rejecting his dominance forever, and a spasm of anger tautened the dark masculine face. 'You cannot morally dictate to me. You are nothing at all to me; Bernard is my friend.'

'Your lover,' Revel corrected harshly, his mouth twisting. 'Until you send him away tomorrow morning, he is your lover. Why dissemble? But soon, you will have a new lover. We both know that, don't we?'

Then she was free, and he was striding back to the gate. Slowly, wearily, Carla went inside. Her cameras had never felt heavier and it was an effort to smile at Bernard who was on his feet and looking bewildered, a tall, slim man with fair curls, vulnerable eyes and a sensitive mouth.

'Carla! I almost thought I was dreaming when I looked up and saw you there, and then you were whisked out of sight in a distinctly nightmarish manner. That was Revel Braden with you, wasn't it?'

'Yes.' She put down her bag and cameras and picked up Pasht who suffered a brief caress before struggling free, intent on beginning the half-hour sulking session that was ritual whenever her mistress had been away overnight. Feeling some explanation was necessary, Carla added, 'He was covering the drought for *The Courant* and *Afrinews*.'

'Not his usual sort of subject,' Bernard observed.

'No.'

'Quite a coincidence, really—I believe Vivienne saw him a few days ago.'

'How is Vivienne?' Carla altered the subject with some relief, and yet she was uneasy. She wanted to ask him if he was aware that Vivienne and Revel were convinced that they were lovers, but she was too inhibited, afraid of embarrrassing him and herself. Her hatred of Revel intensified. He had spoilt her friendship with Bernard. From now on there would always be some constraint, a self-conscious awareness that others too might mistake their relationship as Revel had done.

'She's away at a health farm,' Bernard answered her question with a reserved smile. 'Carrot juice and a lettuce leaf three times a day, saunas, facials, leg-waxing, the works.'

'And Justine?' Carla collapsed into a chair.

'I hope, at home with our housekeeper.' His smile had faded. 'Hell, I just don't know what to do for the best. I must be the world's lousiest father. She's palpably miserable, and no solution I come up with makes any difference. I suggested to her that she might be happier at a nice boarding school and we had another scene, with her accusing me of trying to get rid of her and slamming doors all through the house. I know she's no longer with the crowd who introduced her to liquor, motorbikes and general hellraising last year, but whoever her friends are now, she won't bring them home but goes out to meet them . . . Sometimes I wonder if she's ashamed of our wealth. Perhaps I was wrong to send her to a state school, but I thought it would benefit her more to be one of a majority.'

Carla shook her head. 'Why do you always look for the blame in yourself, Bernard? Can't she be suffering from normal growth pains, asserting her independence?' Privately, though, she was sure her home circumstances did aggravate the girl's unhappiness, but it seemed to her that the responsibility lay more with Vivienne than Bernard. She could hardly say so, however, as Bernard never criticised his wife, or even spoke of her in a personal context. She sat up straighter. 'Shall I make us some coffee?'

'No, thanks, Carla. It's late and I'm sure you're impatient to get into your darkroom. I meant to be gone before you got home but it's the old story—I just sat down and closed my eyes for a few minutes, and next thing, I was fathoms deep. Soothing company, Pasht.' His tired brown eyes smiled. 'But since we have met, would you like to come sailing at Hout Bay on Sunday? I think Vivienne has something on that day, and Justine isn't interested, of course.'

Carla hesitated, remembering Revel's warning. He had had no right to dictate to her, and a sudden mood of defiance made her eyes sparkle now. He needed to be taught a lesson, and she would not be placing herself in any danger, since she had no intention of ever again allowing him to manipulate her into a situaton where he was free to harass her without interference.

'I'd love to, Bernard,' she said.

And Revel Braden could think what he liked when he found out.

CHAPTER THREE

CARLA saw Revel again the following Tuesday morning.

The weekly discussion Alastair Carmichael had with his regular staffers in his office had just broken up and Carla was lingering, talking at her friend Marigold Vibor's desk, when Revel, in cream denims and casual green shirt, strode through the open plan office, making for Alastairs' private sanctum.

Instinctively, Carla swung round to face Marigold so that her back was the only view Revel would have of her, and she was relieved that Marigold's normally observant pansy-coloured eyes failed to note the strangeness of her action. The older girl was too busy following Revel's progress through the room.

'That is what I call a presence,' Marigold stated lasciviously. 'He sweeps through here like an electric storm, leaving the atmosphere crackling with vitality. Dead sexy, too, utterly charming when he wants to be and with that look of hell in his eyes to add an element of danger. An irresistible combination. How did you get on with him in Zululand?'

'I didn't,' Carla said tonelessly, a hint of apricot in her cheeks.

'No, I don't suppose you did.' Marigold eyed her thoughtfully. 'You've never wanted excitement, have you?'

'Not his sort of excitement anyway,' Carla retorted drily, anxious to change the subject. 'My work provides all the excitement I want.'

'You're unnatural. Oh, damn,' Marigold added as a tube of ash dropped off her cigarette contained in one of the affectedly long holders she collected, and fell between the keys of her typewriter. 'What's exciting about this assignment to photograph that jet at Ysterplaat this afternoon, for instance? I don't know how you stand it. It may be very flattering to receive a special invitation from the Defence Force but you'll only be allowed to photograph what they want you to photograph. Me, I'm not permitted in there at all. They're scared of me.'

Carla smiled at her smug expression. Marigold cherished her reputation as a thorn in the flesh of those in power.

'You'll be banned altogether one of these days.'

'So? It could lead to an offer from the *Washington Post* or *Newsweek*.' Marigold laughed wickedly and ran her fingers through the dark curls she had treated with henna. Her eyes slid past Carla. 'That was quick. Hi, Braden, slumming?'

'Your chip is showing, Vibor,' Revel commented, with his quick charming smile, but the look he gave Carla was glittery and hostile.

Marigold shrugged. 'You've got some sway with Nathaniel Nash. Tell me, when is he going to let me join the beating heart of his empire?'

'*The Courant?* When you stop being controversial simply for the sake of it and learn to be truly objective. He wants an original Marigold Vibor, not an imitation Orianna Fallaci,' Revel informed her with a cruelty that made Carla wince, although Marigold merely laughed. He turned to her, enclosing her arm in a steely grip and she felt the blood draining from her face. 'I want a word with you.'

'Watch it, Carla,' Marigold called after them as he steered her away. 'He's probably going to tell you you're an imitation Margaret Bourke-White!'

'I should be so lucky,' Carla murmured ambiguously as Revel marched her through the office, attracting considerable attention.

'Well, she also started out as an industrial photographer before moving on to other things,' Revel drawled.

'So there's hope for me yet,' she added bitterly. 'Except that you don't think I've got the courage.'

'Evidently you haven't got the courage to part with Bernard Franck either,' he condemned sharply. They were out in the corridor now and he shepherded her towards the lifts. 'I did warn you, Carla. Vivienne told me you spent Sunday with him.'

Sunday, a serene blue and gold day, spent idyllically on Bernard's yacht. Carla tried to free her arm as Revel pressed the button to summon the lift, but his hold was unbreakable, hurting her and sending a searingly sensuous tide of heat coursing through her body.

'Vivienne told you,' she repeated sarcastically. 'Because Bernard told her. Why shouldn't he? He has nothing to hide.'

'Still protesting your innocence?' he taunted, the look in his eyes as scorching as his touch as he inspected her breathtakingly perfect figure, its loveliness enhanced by the simplicity of her outfit, a sleeveless pale olive T-shirt tucked into short off-white culottes which she wore with matching espadrilles laced about her slender ankles.

'Well, doesn't it ever occur to you that you might be wrong?' she challenged. 'That you might actually be making a mistake?'

'No,' he said tersely, pushing her into the lift that had arrived. 'I saw that inanely tender smile you couldn't help when you found him waiting for you the other night.'

As the doors slid shut he released her and pressed the ground-floor button. Alone with him in such a confined space, Carla's nervousness escalated unbearably, making her heart hammer painfully and her pulses race.

She swallowed and said, 'Where are we going? I wasn't ready to leave the office yet.'

'With your cameras all slung about you?' Revel derided. 'You've got a lecture at U.C.T. very shortly and an assignment to Ysterplaat this afternoon. I asked Alastair how your day was organised. You're free tonight, though, and I happen to know you're not seeing Bernard because he's taking his wife and daughter out to dinner—I suppose to appease them after his recent neglect. So you'll have dinner with me.'

Carla's fine eyebrows rose superciliously. 'You have such a charming way of asking for a date.'

'I'm not asking you for anything. I'm telling you.'

'But I can still refuse.'

'Can you, Carla?' His voice was silken. 'Do you want to risk my informing Nathaniel Nash that you're having an affair with a married man? You know how straitlaced the old dictator is, and he expects his employees to live as virtuously as he does.'

'That's blackmail.'

'Yes, it is.' He smiled unkindly.

Carla was silent. The feeling in the pit of her stomach had no connection with the swift descent of the lift. It was a combination of sick excitement and melting warmth, utterly debilitating, and she hated him for awakening such feelings in her.

Bitter anger surged in her, but she controlled it, thinking rapidly. If it came to the point, she could provide proof for Nathaniel Nash that she was innocent of the sin of which Revel accused her, but, impulsively, driven by resentment, she decided to teach him a lesson. He needed to learn that he could be wrong, and she would just have to develop the necessary callousness to disregard possible embarrassment to Bernard and get him to explain their relationship to Revel. He would have to believe Bernard. Meanwhile, she would play along. . . .

'I don't want to lose my job,' she admitted dully, glancing up at him out of the corners of her eyes and

suppressing an urge to strike him when she saw the
gleam of triumph in his slanting blue-green eyes.

'Then be ready at seven-thirty and I'll pick you up.'

'All right.' A thought struck her. 'Where ... where
will we be going?'

'Somewhere public, Carla,' he reassured her sardonically, as if he had read her sudden fear.
'Unfortunately, my house is undergoing a complete
face-lift and is unfit for entertaining at present, and my
cottage down at the tip of the Peninsula is too far
away—and I wouldn't dream of asking you to cook
dinner for me.'

'You're right, I might get my hands on some arsenic.'

His smile was brief and mocking. The lift had
reached the ground floor and he allowed her to precede
him out before saying, 'So I'll see you at seven-thirty
then.'

'I'll look forward to it,' Carla retorted ironically.

She stood still to watch him walk out into the street.
He was so tall and dark, an alien being, and there was
so much power in that lithe, muscled body, despite his
leanness. A deep fluttering was assailing her stomach
and there was a tingling sensation along the insides of
her thighs as, against her will, she was caught up in the
violent memory of his ruthless kisses. She couldn't help
wondering and, somehow, knowing, what it would feel
like to experience the length of his body against hers,
without the barrier of clothes. She could visualise him
now, imagine the sensation—Dear God, how had she
ever thought she could cope with him and successfully
teach him a lesson, when he affected her like this?

By half past seven that evening, Carla was almost
paralysed with nerves, and knew a childish urge not to
open the door when Revel arrived, wishing she could
hide away and pretend she wasn't there.

He looked sophisticated and exciting in a lightweight
suit, but that primitive element was still very much in

evidence, especially when he inspected her with a sardonic smile and she saw the sensuous fire kindling in his unusual eyes.

She felt herself flushing and growing self-conscious under such merciless scrutiny, though just a few minutes ago her mirror had told her that she was looking her best tonight. The shining brown hair across her brow had been tended with a hotbrush so that its layers were attractively feathered, and she had used more make-up than usual, elongating her eyes with the skilful use of eyeshadows in natural colours and applying lots of mascara, and she had used a glossy lipstick in a warm shade that harmonised perfectly with the deep, rich apricot colour of her strapless silk dress. The dress was utterly simple, low enough to reveal the upper swell of her breasts but not so low as to make her uncomfortable—except now, when a pair of blue-green eyes rested on the creamy skin. Her slim shoulders gleamed with a magnolia pallor and about the base of her slender neck and circling one wrist were discreet twists of gold, while plain, tiny gold studs gleamed in her earlobes; her high-heeled sandals were strappy, fragile frivolities and her evening bag was a flat gold envelope.

'I'm encouraged,' Revel drawled after appraising her in silence for some seconds—which felt like minutes to Carla.

'Perhaps unwarrantedly,' she ventured pointedly. 'You did say we were going somewhere public?'

'Meaning it's not for me?' His mouth twisted with an odd sort of humour. 'Still it pleases me. You should always dress so simply. That figure of yours attracts attention on its own merits; you don't need adornment.'

Embarrassed, she changed the subject, awkwardly asking if he wanted a drink before they left, and was relieved when he declined. She didn't want him in her flat—her home and her haven, where she could be quiet and safe, where she escaped from the abrasiveness of the city life which still had its alien aspects to trouble her spirit after all these years. She locked the door, having earlier checked that all windows were proof against any escape attempts by Pasht whom she provided with a litter tray and kept in at night.

Her inherent shyness held her silent during the drive to Sea Point, and Revel made no effort to get her talking. She wore her reserve about her like an invisible but tangible armour. She knew that many people interpreted it as a cold hauteur, and regretted it, but with this man, it might prove an asset. To actually be going out to dinner with him—now it seemed an overwhelmingly foolish step, and she wondered just how he intended the evening to end.

The restaurant was one that featured permanently in media lists of Cape Town's top ten restaurants, usually making the top five, but she had never been there before and its plain but luxurious interior impressed her. Their table offered them privacy while permitting them to observe most of the room, and the waiters were well trained, attentive without being too effusively friendly.

'Are you always so quiet or is it only with me?' Revel asked her over their initial drinks.

'No, not only with you, but perhaps I'm particularly so with you,' she corrected him with faint humour.

'I could find it very restful, once I've stopped finding you so exciting,' he remarked idly, but with a glint in his eyes that warned her of his intentions.

'I wish you didn't find me exciting,' she told him gravely—it made her uncomfortable.

'Believe me, Carla, so do I,' Revel retorted bitterly, his eyes now brooding as they rested on her secretive face. 'I suppose I can't blame Franck. You're very desirable and that quiet manner only adds to the allure because it makes a mystery of you. Do you drop it in the bedroom, or are you one of those ungenerous women who always withhold some secret part of themselves, revealing their bodies but never their souls?'

His words conjured up a crowd of erotic images and deep colour stained her cheeks.

'Are you going to talk in this crude manner all evening?' she wondered and her mortification increased as she heard the husky note in her voice.

'I'd call it candid rather than crude,' he returned, watching her with amusement. 'But I agree, we'd better find some less . . . evocative topic or we'll never make it to the end of the meal.'

Carla was still seething with resentment as their entrée course, Danish blue with avocado, arrived, but gradually her innate politeness asserted itself and she forced herself to respond to his attempts to get her talking. The necessity of choosing a wine to accompany their meal led to a discussion on Cape viticulture and the discovery of a mutual preference for dry whites, while over the next course, an unusual combination of baked fish with fruit, they found they shared an interest in contemporary cinema.

Then, some time later, Carla noticed the light that flared in Revel's eyes as his glance strayed to a table at the other side of the restaurant but directly opposite theirs.

'Take a good look over there, Carla,' he advised harshly.

Her trained photographer's eye followed the direction of his gaze and her audibly indrawn breath was proof of the shock that assailed her when she saw the Francks, looking like the ideal family party save for their various expressions of discontent, unhappiness and boredom.

Briefly, as she turned to look at Revel once more, her face was curiously naked, her eyes wounded and her lips quivering, before anger replaced vulnerability.

'You've done this deliberately, haven't you?' she accused in a low voice. 'You knew they'd be here.'

'Yes,' he admitted, watching her.

'Why?' she demanded with shaky scorn. 'What were you hoping to do—arouse my conscience?'

'Or perhaps accustom Franck to the idea that you are no longer his exclusive property,' Revel supplied with barely contained savagery. 'Since you've evidently found it impossible to end your affair, it looks as if I'm going to have to do it for you.'

'You bastard,' she said very quietly and yet with a wealth of intense feeling.

'Take a good look at that kid, Carla,' he recommended. 'Though it needs less than that to see she's riddled with hang-ups; she can do without the extra aggravation your involvement with her father is causing to her parents' marriage.'

But Carla resolutely refused to look, after a single glance had taken in the fact that Bernard, aware of her presence, was looking miserably perplexed. Diligently, she kept her downcast eyes on her plate, but she was no longer enjoying her meal, excellent though it was. Nausea attacked her and after a few minutes she placed her knife and fork together and declined the sweet course when their waiter reappeared.

'Smile at me, Carla,' Revel ordered sharply when her silence became extended.

'Why should I?' she countered coldly.

'I want your lover to be very sure that he's about to be replaced, and that entails giving the impression that you're enjoying my company.'

'Do you really expect my co-operation?' Carla demanded tartly.

'I think I do.' His hand covered hers which was lying clenched on the damask-covered table top. 'Unless you want that little girl to know that her father is being unfaithful to her mother. In a little while, we're going to

join them for coffee and you're going to give them all
the impression that I'm the man in your life and you're
happy that I should be so.'

'I suppose this is something you and Vivienne Franck
planned between you.'

He smiled sardonically and kept his hand over hers.
A surreptitious glance showed Carla that Bernard was
looking in her direction once more, and she could guess
how the scene would appear to him, a couple holding
hands over the table, Revel leaning forward a little.

She wished she had the nerve to stand up and walk
out on him. I should be uncaring, she thought
yearningly, but she knew that even the smallest
dilemmas in life would never be dismissed without
intense agonising on her part. Things mattered too
much to her.

The invitation to join the Francks for coffee was
relayed by a waiter and Carla stood up with reluctance.
Revel's guiding hand at her back was possessive and an
insult, yet it weakened her, and inwardly she shook with
a deep, shaming awareness of him as a man, sensual
and dominant.

Vivienne Franck was so beautiful and self-assured
that Carla found it difficult to believe she suspected
Bernard of being unfaithful to her with someone as
ordinary as herself. In a straight black shift and
diamonds, her lovely colouring was shown to advantage,
thick fair hair and a duskily tanned skin making an
unusual combination, while her eyes were the bluest
Carla had ever seen, deep inky pools. She must be in
her mid-thirties, perhaps ten years younger than
Bernard, and her figure remained superb, for her height
robbed a full bust and womanly hips of any suggestion
of matronliness.

'Enjoy your meal?' she questioned Carla perfunctorily
but didn't wait for an answer, one of those women with
little time for their own sex. Her amazing eyes darted

restlessly between the two men, and her tongue flickered provocatively over pouting lips as she focused on Revel. 'And you, Revel? Of course, you come here quite often when you're in town. I like it myself, but I could have done with a party, instead of just the three of us.'

'I hope Carla and I are some compensation, then,' Revel murmured urbanely, having greeted Bernard with a brief inclination of his head. He smiled at the fourteen-year-old girl who could no more take her eyes off him than the women could. 'Hullo, Justine, how are you doing?'

She opened her mouth to reply but her mother cut her short with a dismissive laugh. 'Oh, she has been gorging herself on those profiteroles. . . . Honestly! She complains about being fat, but keeps right on eating. A real little glutton.'

It was appallingly cruel and the poor child went scarlet, not knowing where to look. Carla's own cheeks grew warm with embarrassed sympathy. It was true that Justine was overweight and her lemon yellow dress, the height of fashion for the high-school set that summer, was a mistake. It must be so demoralising for the offspring of attractive parents to be plump and plain, and her hair was mousey where her parents were both fair, while her eyes were a lighter brown than Bernard's and myopic, making Carla suspect she was supposed to wear glasses but was reluctant to add to what she probably regarded as her overall unattractiveness. She wondered if anyone had suggested contact lenses, but she knew they sometimes proved unsuitable for sensitive eyes.

'Have you ordered coffee?' Revel asked Bernard, ignoring the girl's discomfiture, probably the best thing he could have done, Carla reluctantly conceded.

'We were waiting to see what you wanted,' Bernard explained. 'I know Carla likes Irish coffee after a meal. You?'

A spasm of anger tautened Revel's face and he answered irritably. Carla supposed he thought Bernard was being tactless, drawing attention to his familiarity with her tastes.

She wished herself a thousand miles away, and sat in silence when her Irish coffee was brought to her, sipping it slowly but not enjoying it quite as much as usual because of the nervous tension that made her stomach churn. Justine too was silent, wearing a sulky expression, but the other three had the polished sophistication necessary to ignore the various hostile currents flowing round the table, although Bernard occasionally lapsed into a thoughtful silence. Once, while Revel and Vivienne were discussing a political issue, he looked questioningly at Carla, arching his eyebrows, but she shook her head very slightly. A sudden tension in Revel, sitting beside her, made her aware that he had noticed, and probably misinterpreted, the tiny exchange, and her resentment and unhappiness increased.

'I suppose you'll be taking off for some trouble-spot again any day now, Revel?' Vivienne was saying, and the barely concealed distaste in her voice captured Carla's attention.

Revel replied noncommittally for, as she had already realised, he didn't like talking about his work and his face was hard and inscrutable as he returned Vivienne's look—Vivienne's look! Carla felt shaken. There was a hot, sick hunger in the woman's eyes as they rested greedily on Revel's appearance, devouring him. . . .

She loves him, Carla thought, and she recalled Revel saying that there was no such thing as a platonic friendship between men and women. He had evidently spoken from experience.

Were they having an affair? A host of unpleasant suspicions came crowding in on Carla, darkening her mind. She had been naïve. Knowing that Revel and

Vivienne had grown up together, she had assumed that the relationship between them was one of ordinary friendship. Now such an assumption seemed laughably innocent. Put two such vibrantly attractive people together and there had to be an explosive chemical reaction.

She looked at Vivienne contemplatively, pitying her a little. It must be hell to love a man who pursued such a career as Revel's, always flying off into danger where the rational majority would flee it.

Departure noises were beginning to be made, so she stood up and excused herself, making for the discreetly concealed passage leading to the Ladies. She had her evening bag open on the console counter in front of the mirror while she renewed her lipstick, when Vivienne walked in.

'I just wanted to say . . . thanks for helping out with our little bit of . . . camouflage.' The blonde woman appraised Carla's reflection and then glanced at her own with open satisfaction. 'Though, I must say, I'm surprised Revel should have chosen you, when you're so close to Bernard. I was expecting one of his other playmates, Noelle Malherbe or someone.'

'I'm sorry?' Carla turned her head to give her an uncomprehending look, but Vivienne was too caught up in herself to notice, a self-absorbed woman who didn't want to hear, only to tell.

'I suppose I have been a little self-indulgent, and seen too much of Revel,' she went on, tipping her head back, her eyes half-closed as she surveyed her mirrored image, and to Carla, there was someting obscene about the pose, like a public display of intimacy, because she was sure that Vivienne was reliving some hour spent making love with Revel. 'But, God, he enslaves me, and he's away so often, so who can blame me? I'm afraid Bernard was beginning to suspect, so we had to head him off quickly.'

Recalling Bernard's recent, growing unhappines, though he had never confided in her and she had put it down to overwork, homesick longing for the old, simple Karoo life and concern about his daughter, Carla could now quite easily believe it.

Her voice sounded oddly strangled as she asked, 'But if you ... if it's Revel, wouldn't it be better to let Bernard know, so that you could be free to ... to——'

'And have him divorce me?' Vivienne's eyes flew open and she laughed scornfully. 'He would, you know, if he found out. He thinks I'm no use as a mother, so consideration for Justine wouldn't stop him. And don't mention the generous allowance he'd undoubtedly give me. That isn't what I want. I want to be Bernard Franck's wife; it's my environment, part of my personality and it gains me entrée in certain circles ... Bernard is for security, Revel for ... excitement.'

The feverish, reminiscent glitter returned to the inky eyes as she mentioned Revel, and Carla felt appalled.

'And so I'm being used to ... to convince Bernard that Revel isn't interested in you?' She had to force the words out and her knuckles showed white as she gripped the edge of the counter.

There was a flash of something in Vivienne's eyes, as if she disliked her particular choice of words, and perhaps they were crude, but she couldn't have phrased it differently.

'Good heavens, surely Revel warned you? Or perhaps he didn't. Like most men, he wants the best of both worlds. I'm sorry he has used you like this. . . . He knows he can't give me the life I want, the security of marriage, but he's taking a lot from me, our times together are like nothing I've known before, and he feels he owes it to me in return for that to ensure that I'm not deprived of my background security through my liaison with him. . . . You won't tell Bernard, will you? I know you're fond of him but you don't actually want him for yourself? Ignorance is bliss and by co-operating, you'll be helping to keep three people happy.'

'I won't tell Bernard. It's none of my business.' Carla just wanted to wash her hands of the whole sordid, complex imbroglio into which she had been dragged against her will.

'Thanks.' Seeing Carla about to leave the cloakroom, Vivienne added, 'Incidentally, this whole set-up was Revel's idea, not mine. You've a right to be angry at being used, so if you do want to get out, I won't blame you. Frankly, I think he'd have done better and convinced Bernard more fully if he'd brought someone like Noelle Malherbe. No offence, Carla, but you're not really Revel's type.'

But he wants me, Carla thought, and then—but wanting isn't loving.

Her steps slowed as she walked across the restaurant. Vivienne was the woman he loved, all others merely sex objects. And he must love her a lot, to be prepared to go to these devious lengths to keep her marriage intact. She sensed that personally he would have little use for concealment since he was not a man who cared what others thought of him, but for Vivienne's sake, knowing she needed the security of her marriage behind her, he was willing to engage in subterfuge.

She wondered if he really believed she was having an affair with Bernard, or if he had been using it as an excuse. But for what? It seemed clear that Vivienne had no such suspicion, but possibly Revel had misread her relationship with the engineering tycoon, and now thought he was, in a sense, killing two birds with one stone. Loving Vivienne, wanting what she wanted, he was ensuring that all threats to her precious marriage were removed.

She hated them both, she thought wildly, made bitterly angry by Revel's machinations. Her anger was a tangible thing, filling the interior of the car when he drove her back to Gardens. To have been used. . . . Somewhere was a core of hurt, but her anger was preponderant.

'Well?' Revel challenged after a few minutes.

'Well, what?' Carla snapped.

'I think this evening met with tolerable success, don't you? Bernard Franck is very definitely wondering what's going on between us——'

'Oh, spare me any more of your hypocrisy,' Carla interrupted tautly. 'That wasn't the main purpose of this evening, was it? I know why you engineered the whole thing, and it certainly wasn't for Justine's sake. God, for a while you had me believing that you might actually have a single redeeming quality—the fact that you were sorry for her and cared about her feelings. I know better now. I know for whose sake you did it.'

'Oh, you do?'

'Yes!'

'And what are you going to do about it?' Revel enquired casually.

'Nothing. I want out—I'm getting out,' she told him. 'You have no right to use me like this because, I repeat, I am not having an affair with Bernard Franck.'

'Sorry, Carla, but I don't believe you,' he stated in a hard voice. 'I saw the way he was looking at you tonight—like one dog watches the bone that has been given to another. He was sick with wanting you, and jealous as hell because he thinks you've started being unfaithful to him.'

'Bernard is not my lover,' she declared again in a voice that broke, for quite suddenly she was close to tears, desperately wanting him to believe her, and hurt because he didn't.

'Give me one good reason, if he's not, why he presumably has a key to your flat and was waiting for you at that late hour we got back from Zululand last week,' Revel invited her silkily. 'Not just for a chat, that's for sure.'

'I had left the key hidden for him,' she explained tiredly. 'He had been in to feed my cat because the neighbour who usually does it was in hospital. He sat down and, because he'd been working late and was tired, he fell asleep.'

His laughter touched her like darts dipped in poison. 'You'll have to think of something better than that, sweetheart. Franck is virtually a millionaire and a busy man. Men like that don't go around feeding single girl's cats for them unless there's somewhat more than friendship between them.'

'Bernard does,' she flared. 'He likes that sort of thing, simple, ordinary tasks that mean something. We're like that, where he and I come from, the Karoo. We don't demand sophistication every minute of the day.'

'Oh, drop it, Carla,' he adjured irritably, 'Do you love him?'

'No.'

'He loves you.' He laughed again, a derisive sound that made her tense with resentment. 'I'll bet you my only chance of salvation that the minute he can get rid of Vivienne and Justine tonight, he'll be on the phone to you, wanting to know why you were out with me.'

There was no point in protesting, she realised wearily. He never believed anything she told him, so she might as well keep silent.

When they reached her flat, he got out of the car and walked with her through the gate and to the door, where she turned after extracting her key from her bag.

'I won't thank you——'

'I'm coming in with you,' Revel cut her short, taking the key from her fingers and inserting it in the lock.

Fear quickened in her, making her voice slightly breathless as she said, 'You're bigger and stronger than me, so I don't suppose I can stop you, but I'd rather you didn't.'

He pushed open the door and returned the key to her, saying, 'I want to be here when Franck rings.'

'He won't.' She switched on the hall light and moved towards the lounge where she did the same. The more lights, the better; darkness was too intimate.

'He will.'

Revel had followed her into the lounge, and she turned to look at him, but found herself unable to meet his eyes. A combination of nervousness and her habitual shyness was making her incapable of speech, and her creamy face was even paler than usual.

'Stop looking like that, darling. I may make love to you but I won't rape you. I won't need to, will I?' Revel taunted softly, but made no move to touch her. He glanced at Pasht, who watched him with slit-eyed suspicion from her usual position. 'So this is the cat. . . . Your alibi.'

'That's Pasht,' Carla confirmed faintly, standing in the middle of the room and feeling helpless.

'Pasht, or Bastet, Isis's cat-headed daughter,' he reflected with a slight smile. 'Quite original, Carla.'

'Not really, if you remember that the common English Puss comes from the Egyptian Pasht,' she reminded him lightly, but her downcast hazel eyes were dark with trepidation and her vulnerable lips were quivering.

'Oh, for God's sake!' Revel exclaimed impatiently, raking her with an irritated glance. 'Go and make us some coffee, and accustom yourself to the idea that from now on it will always be me here with you, not Franck. You'll get used to me in time.'

She couldn't answer—she could hardly breathe. She had to gulp to inhale any air at all and, with an inarticulate little sound, she turned and walked blindly towards her small kitchen.

Her chaotic thoughts refused to sort themselves out and the popping, bubbling noise of the percolator was a sound that drove her mad. A hundred urgent, unanswerable questions churned through her mind. If he attempted to make love to her, how was she to resist him?

Her mouth curved bitterly. He only wanted her; it was Vivienne Franck he loved. Dear God, it was degrading to be desired simply because she had been cursed with the sort of figure that featured in male fantasies. . . . She must not lose sight of that knowledge, or she would be lost.

When she carried the pretty wooden tray through to the lounge, Revel had removed his jacket and was sitting on the brown sofa with its deep gold cushions, trading stares with Pasht, and as Carla put the tray down on the coffee table, the cups rattling because she was shaking, the telephone began to ring.

CHAPTER FOUR

'I'LL answer that.'

Before Carla could react, Revel had stood up and crossed to the telephone which had its own Cape yellowwood table under the interior circular stairs which led up to her studio.

'Yes?'

She stood watching him warily, noting the hard, quick smile of satisfaction he gave as he listened to the caller. He was dark, his well-cut hair almost black, his skin deeply tanned by the sun that shone on the world's most troubled countries, so many of them in Africa and the Middle East, and there was a faint shadow to his strong jaw. Against such darkness, his eyes were brilliant, reminding her of the destructive sea, beautiful and ruthless.

Her attention drawn by the words he was speaking into the telephone, she stared at him, hatred deepening.

His voice low, suggestive and oddly elated, Revel was saying, 'Sorry, but it really is inconvenient for you to speak to Carla just now. And, Franck, I'd appreciate it if you stayed out of her life from now on. I'll admit it's a flaw in my nature, but I do tend to be possessive about my women.'

Sheer, blind rage carried her across the room as he replaced the receiver. To hear herself described like an article of property belonging to him was intolerable, his glittering smile more than she could bear. Her right arm swung back, describing a horizontal arc, and then shot forward, her small clenched fist connecting with his jaw with satisfying violence.

She fully expected Revel to retaliate, but instead of

hitting her, he placed his hands on her arms and hauled her brutally up against him. Instantly she was pierced by a sharp, sexual excitement, her pupils dilating as she looked fearfully up into his dark, implacable face.

'Do you always reply with such childish gestures when you're proved to be a liar?' His mouth twisted derisively. 'I was right, wasn't I? I knew he'd have to phone you. . . . Never lie to me again, Carla.'

His mouth found hers, stifling her cry of pain. Her lips were crushed beneath the grinding force of his for what felt like aeons, and she could only cling helplessly to him, her fingers digging into his rippling, straining shoulder muscles for as long as the assault lasted.

At last he raised his head to look down into her tear-wet eyes.

'What's the matter, darling?' he mocked. 'Does it hurt to know Franck is lost to you? You'll get over it. . . . You shall have a new lover, and I'll make you forget him.'

His mouth touched hers again, and she felt her self-control slipping away from her under this further onslaught of passion. His arms were steel bands across her back and his tongue probed the soft inner flesh of her mouth until a tearing sob of despair and desire broke from her. Her vision had darkened, as if to match the benighted nature of their passion. Sensing the desperation and violence in him, an answering frenzy rose in her, making her fingers tremble violently as they raked through his dark hair.

She wanted him, ah, God, she wanted him! But to let him make love to her, feeling as he did, would be to descend to a nadir of shame from which she would never be able to extricate herself again.

'Don't do this to me, Revel,' she begged brokenly as he steered her towards the sofa, both of them heedless of the little questioning miaow that came from a perplexed Pasht.

'Don't be a fool,' he retorted. 'Accept it, Carla, face up to reality for once in your life. We have this . . . this need of each other, however much we may despise ourselves for it. How long do you think it can be denied? And look at it this way, by getting together, we'll be freeing the Franck marriage of a dual threat— because it's not only Bernard who is endangering that marriage, Vivienne is doing her share as well.'

He pushed her down on to the sofa among the soft golden cushions, and joined her there. Carla wanted time to assimilate and analyse his words, but all thought receded as Revel's mouth covered hers again and all that was left to her was a scandalously erotic need.

She was a molten mass of sensation, writhing in his arms as every kiss and caress added to her shuddering excitement and she moaned impatiently as she felt Revel's fingers at the zip that ran down one side of her dress. She wore no bra and Revel raised her a little to tug the silken material down as far as her hips, then drew back to look at her as she collapsed against the cushions once more.

His harsh indrawn breath was a tribute to the beauty of her body, and the look in his eyes was that of a man gone beyond reason. Shy colour crept into Carla's cheek's. No man had ever seen her body like this before, and that this stranger should be the first to look at her. . . .

'Don't,' she pleaded, but Revel was deaf to the voice of innocence, caressing her with hard, hot eyes, their colour turned to pure, glittery turquoise.

His hands moved to touch the proud breasts and they swelled painfully against his palms, and then his sure, skilled fingers were teasing her hardening nipples to tautness. He continued to stroke and massage her aching breasts for long, delirious moments before lowering his head, and from beneath heavy eyelids,

Carla saw in his darkness against her creamy flesh a
strangely poignant, erotic beauty. Then his mouth was
touching one agonisingly erect pinnacle, kissing,
caressing, his tongue circling over the dark ruched flesh,
flickering and darting until her inhibitions melted and
she could no longer contain a hoarse, throbbing cry of
purest pleasure.

'You're beautiful ... perfect,' Revel was muttering
heatedly as he transferred his mouth to the other nipple,
lips massaging the hard hot evidence of her arousal. His
hands closed over her hips and slid down taking her
dress with them, so that she was nearly naked. His
fingers stroked the satiny length of her thighs and then
up again to her stomach and slender waist and down
once more, lightly skimming the region covered by her
little coffee-coloured lace-trimmed panties.

Breathing fast, unevenly, he eventually raised his
head to look at her, his dark perspiration-beaded face
contorting with some intense emotion as he noted her
glazed, half-closed eyes, the bright pulsing loveliness of
her mouth and the flush of passion that lay across her
breasts.

'God, I want you,' he groaned harshly as he
discarded his loosened tie and rapidly undid the buttons
of his cream shirt.

'Revel!' The small cry was part shame, part appeal.

'God!'

He bent over her, his eyes on her mouth, and Carla
arched beneath him until she was touching him,
rubbing her breasts against the dark, softly curling hair
that covered his chest. Revel's breathing became even
more laboured, rapid tremors rippling through his taut
body as he claimed her mouth in another endless kiss.
All control was gone and a long, continuous moaning
sound came from deep in his throat as Carla wrapped
her arms about him, shaking with the force of the desire
he had aroused in her.

'Ah, but you drive me insane!' His voice was thick, impeded, as he trailed kisses over the slender column of her neck and the smoothness of her shoulders. 'Forget about Franck, Carla, don't think about him. It's me you want tonight. . . . Say it, tell me you want me!'

But his reference to Bernard brought a return of sanity, and Carla's arms fell away from him, her body growing rigid with rejection as she remembered all that lay between them, the mistrust and hostility that ran through all their passion like a glaring flaw in an otherwise richly beautiful fabric.

He was using her. Now she was able to reflect on what he had said earlier about the Franck marriage, his admission that Vivienne too was contributing her share to its possible breakdown. It occurred to Carla then that perhaps Revel was actually trying to give Vivienne up, and using her as a substitute—still using her! And she couldn't let him. She wanted him, with shaming hunger, the ache of desire gathering and becoming a hollowness concentrated at the receptive core of her femininity, but the knowledge that she was being made use of was an intolerably agonising humiliation. She couldn't bear the pain and shame of it. . . .

'No! Revel, please stop!' she beseeched urgently, her voice jerky and uneven with the threat of tears. 'For pity's sake, don't do this to me!'

'I must!'

The dark tortured face above hers was sheened with perspiration, and his eyes blazed with a passion almost daemonic in its intensity. Carla knew he was incapable of stopping what was going to happen, gone way beyond the bounds of self-control, and she realised it was partly her fault. She should have resisted him earlier instead of responding until he was maddened by the desire she could feel surging in his body.

At the thought, anguish flooded her being, and she pleaded with hoarse desperation—'Then please, Revel, at least believe that I'm telling you the truth about Bernard. He has never been my lover.'

'You cold-blooded bitch! Even at a moment like this you can remember to lie.'

By sheer chance, she had found the words to douse his desire. He wrenched himself away from her and sat on the edge of the sofa, head bent while his elbows rested on his thighs, his hands hanging limply between his knees.

Carla stared at him, noticing that his breathing was still rapid and that the hand he eventually lifted to fasten the buttons of his shirt contained a faint tremor. Abruptly he turned his head to look at her and she saw that he was in some sort of agony, his eyes full of a bleak savagery, his mouth a harsh gash and the dark skin stretched tautly over his facial bones.

'I'm sorry,' she whispered, horrified.

'Why should you be?' Revel grated with bitter mockery. 'You've got your own way, for tonight at least. Oh, you want me with your body, I know, it's not something you can help, the way your flesh reacts to mine. . . . But in your mind and your heart, Bernard Franck is still the only lover you want.'

'No——'

'Passion is truth, Carla, one of the eternal verities. I'm no longer in the mood to make love to you tonight, but when I do, as I will, it will be pure passion, with none of your lies to mar it.'

He stood up and, perhaps sensing the lingering violence in him, the watchful Pasht leapt from her special chair and crept, belly almost touching the pale gold carpet, beneath the coffee table. But Revel's only action was to pick up his jacket and tie before turning to look at Carla once more, his eyes narrowing with cruel mockery as he watched her trembling fingers struggling to hitch her dress up over her breasts.

She swung her feet on to the floor and stood up to deal with the long zip, before giving him a bitter look.

'Passion is truth, you tell me. My God, you're a hypocrite,' she accused. 'When you were using me. ... My passion was more honest than yours, though I'm still deeply ashamed of letting you make me feel that way. You're dead right, passion is truth! And I told you the truth. I couldn't lie ... I wouldn't! Think about that, Revel, because unless you can believe it, I don't want to see you again.'

'Nevertheless, you will.' With an impatient movement of his shoulders, he turned and strode across the room. Carla followed him into the hall and when he reached the door he faced her again, pulling her towards him and laying a proprietorial hand over her silk-covered breasts, making her gasp as the flesh tautened and a pool of heat collected in the pit of her stomach once more and began to spread itself through all her being. 'I don't want you seeing Franck again. Is that clear? I may not have actually taken you yet, but you're mine, Carla. You know that, don't you? You belong to me.'

'You bastard,' she whispered through kiss-swollen lips, hating the treacherous impulses of her body that made her want to move closer to him and lean against the hard strength she found so exciting.

Revel smiled, knowing perfectly what he was doing to her, and his eyes gleamed with derision behind the screen of dark eyelashes which, in a man, were unfairly long.

'I'll be contacting you.'

He opened the door and went outside, and Carla quickly slammed it shut after him, her fingers clumsy as she made sure it was locked and chained. She was shaking badly with reaction as she returned to the lounge and sank to her knees beside the sofa on which she had so recently twisted and turned beneath the hard weight of Revel's heated body. She buried her face in her arms, sobbing uncontrollably until a questioning 'purrp' made her look up to find Pasht on the sofa, looking at her with faintly indignant enquiry.

'Oh, Pasht!' Carla flung an arm over the cat but there was no comfort to be had from her pet tonight. Unaccustomed to so much emotion, Pasht struggled away and sprang lithely to the back of the sofa where she sat, offendingly washing herself, studiously ignoring Carla.

Carla drew a shuddering breath, expelling it with a weary sigh. She was beginning to shiver, cold despite the warmth of the summer night. She stood up, offering a conciliatory hand to Pasht who condescended to give it a brief lick followed by a reluctant, rusty purr as Carla rubbed her gently behind the ears.

'What am I going to do, Pasht?' she whispered with a tremulous smile.

There was only one answer and she knew it already. She must refuse to have anything further to do with Revel Braden.

Briefly she wished she could have been like Marigold Vibor, able to embark on an affair without too much soul-searching and walk away unscathed when desire had run its course, but she wasn't made that way and she couldn't change herself. Revel was dangerous to her, he could destroy her, and her sole defence in future would be to avoid him.

Any deliberate avoidance proved unnecessary, however. A couple of days later, Carla learnt that less than twenty-four hours after she had last seen him, Revel had flown to Chad where trouble had erupted.

She should have been relieved, but instead she found herself constantly thinking about him and, with a strange feeling of guilt, she scrutinised *The Courant* every day and read every word of the copy he filed. After a few days, she admitted to herself that she was afraid—afraid for Revel.

It was ironic, she realised, that she could care so

much about the safety of someone she hated. If she hated him. She didn't understand him, but in some odd way she felt close to him. She knew him. She knew him as a complex, intelligent man with a dark, tormented side to his nature that made him restless and reckless, and that was why she feared for him.

After three weeks, the Chad situation became quieter, but Revel moved on to cover a similar outbreak of violence in Ghana, so the fear that fretted at Carla remained unalleviated. As if it wasn't enough to be haunted by the prospect of his being killed, she remained tormented by the memory of the sensual fire he had aroused in her, a fire which burned ever more fiercely despite the absence of anything to feed on. She would not allow him to take her and use her and then go on his way, leaving her shattered, as her knowledge of herself told her she would be. She would not give him the opportunity to destroy her.

She was glad that her work kept her so busy. There was her part-time lecturing, plus assignments all over South Africa as well as to other African countries, though less troubled than those from which Revel's reports still came. She flew to Botswana, Malawi and Zambia to photograph some impressive industrial projects, and at home in Cape Town, between her normal work she was more willing than previously to help out with subjects that didn't actually fall within her sphere. She desperately needed to keep busy, because that way she had less time to think and less unused energy left to keep her awake at night.

Additionally, she welcomed any extra work because it gave her an excuse to see less of Bernard Franck. His telephone call after seeing her dining with Revel had shaken her a little and she wonderd if Revel might have some justification for at least one of his accusations. That telephone call, coming at the time it did, implied some emotional involvement, a possessiveness on

Bernard's part, and if he did feel something more than friendship for her, then it seemed kinder to give him less opportunity of seeing her.

Gradually, during the six weeks following that evening in Sea Point, Carla tactfully managed to cut down their regular meetings, regretting the extra loneliness it entailed for her and the sense of being cut off from all who shared in and understood the desert background which made her an alien plant in the city environment, but resolute in wanting to spare him hurt.

Nothing he said or did added to the suspicion that Revel might have been correct in saying Bernard loved her, and yet Carla sensed a change in him. There was a new sadness in the way he watched her, which he did more than he had previously, and he was even more reserved than usual. He never questioned her about Revel, or referred to the evening she had been out with him, and nor did he ever mention that telephone call, and Carla's own deep reticence prevented her from raising the subject. If they discussed any personal matter at all, it was Bernard's continuing anxiety about his daughter.

It was six weeks after that dinner in Sea Point that it became necessary for Carla to make contact with Bernard when, for the last two, she had seen nothing of him, having been able to turn down an invitation to go sailing with him the previous weekend, thanks to an assignment in the rapidly expanding Richards Bay on the north coast of Natal.

This weekend, knowing Sunday was Bernard's only reasonably free day and in order have a genuine excuse at hand should he ask her again, she had both startled and gratified Alastair Carmichael by offering to do the photography for a feature Marigold Vibor was preparing on a subject that was really well outside her province. It was one she found distressing and distasteful, yet simultaneously technically rewarding because she was using one of the superb miniature cameras she had found so reliable on a number of jobs.

It was ironic, Carla was to think later, that her manufactured alibi had been directly responsible for the meeting with Bernard which was to have such far-reaching and devastating consequences.

Throughout that Sunday, she and Marigold had trailed round a series of so-called churches, recording the phenomenon that was causing so much comment these days, religion for profit. The rallies, for they were that rather than services, were held mostly in hired halls and lasted for an average of three hours, and the preachers were mostly blandly smiling men with toothpaste commercial smiles who verbally whipped their congregations into a frenzy of religious ecstasy and then urged them to give generously when the great collection drums were taken round.

Carla and Marigold had given an hour each to three different meetings that morning and had attended another in the afternoon, and Carla had found them deeply depressing. One was palpably corrupt, two misguided and one genuine in its naïve good intentions.

'This one is the worst,' Marigold mentioned as they waited for the fifth to get underway that evening. 'This guy has a highly suspect degree, for a start. He has been in the business two years and has already got a virtual mansion on ten acres of ground out of it, where he entertains girls who are still legally minors. Faith-healing is his thing. A couple of months back, a woman nearly died because he told her she was cured and she believed him and threw away her insulin supply. The poor sucker went back and he told her she hadn't been healed because she hadn't truly cast out the evil in her soul. . . . She believed that too, I suppose.'

They were in a vast hall, hemmed in by excited humanity, and Carla felt sick. Her job was merely to take photographs; Marigold had to evaluate what they were witnessing. Her background research had involved interviews with psychologists and the priests, ministers, pastors and dominees of the established churches, but Carla hadn't needed her frequent quotation of them to tell her she was seeing something appallingly cynical.

This preacher, in his forties, was handsome in a plastic way, and gifted in the sort of maniacal rhetoric that inspired one of the most terrifying spectacles in the world, mass hysteria. Carla was frightened, but nobody noticed her taking her photographs; all eyes were on the man before them. It was he whom they had come to worship and adore, and they did so with screams, tears, clapping, stamping and even wild laughter while his acolytes added to the atmosphere of frenzied abandon with dramatic drum rolls and the rattle of tambourines.

The congregation, Carla observed, was predominantly adolescent with a majority of girls, but the elderly were well-represented too, presumably attracted by the promise of healing. It was the girls who aroused her deepest compassion, however, for they were all glaringly infatuated with that smiling man who kept telling them he loved them and wanted to 'save' them. . . .

'Poor things,' she murmured to Marigold under cover of the growing pandemonium. 'But not so poor; they're rich kids, aren't they? Their clothes and jewellery indicate affluent backgrounds. What lack, what hunger brings them here?'

'Listen to what he's saying and you'll understand,' Marigold advised harshly, her dark eyes disgusted as they swivelled back to the preacher.

'And if you prosper and grow rich, take it as a sign that you are chosen. The good things in life are for those who have been saved; want is the lot of the unsaved——'

Carla looked at Marigold again. 'And this, in the Name of a Man who owned no property?'

'Sick, isn't it? It's his theme tune, that material wealth is the reward for virtue.... That psychologist I interviewed reckons that's what appeals to half these people here. They've felt guilty about being rich and he takes away their guilt, justifies their wealth—and urges them to give some of it to him, of course. I managed a look at this lot's record of accounts, I won't say how. Mind-blowing! They pay fortunes for the illusion of virtue he sells them. Got your photos? Then let's go before I throw up.'

'Gladly!'

It was as they were forcing their way through the frenzied throng that she saw Justine Franck. The girl didn't see her. She was high on an excess of emotion, her plain face flushed and impassioned, eyes ecstatic, mouth screaming her adoration.

Carla faltered momentarily, overwhelmed with sympathy for both Justine, and Bernard who was so worried about her. So this was what had replaced the bike boys who had spent her pocket money on liquor; this gross, sordid lie, so much worse, so evil.... By the time Carla had been dropped at her flat, she was half-convinced that Bernard ought to be told of what his daughter was involved in.

She hesitated in the little enclosed courtyard, deliberating the matter. She would feel like an informer if she told Bernard, she knew, and she kept thinking of some famous words of Franklin D. Roosevelt's, about freedom to worship God in one's own way being one of the four essential freedoms.... Wasn't that what Justine was doing? And yet, what she had seen convinced Carla that the girl was in a potentially harmful situation.

She shivered as the wind whipped at the short chalk-coloured wrap-around skirt she wore with a deep rose pink blouse. A hint of autumn had settled on Cape Town now, with darkness falling early and the occasional days when a soft, drifting rain obscured Table Mountain.

She let herself into the flat, having finally decided that she would let Bernard know what she had seen and tell him what the psychologist had told Marigold. He was trying to be a good father and deserved what little help she could give him. Any decision to act on her information would be his.

She dialled his home number after making herself coffee, and a servant put her through to him.

'Carla? I tried to contact you earlier today and got no reply.'

'I was working,' she explained carefully, and quickly told him about what she had seen that evening.

Bernard was first concerned, then horrified, but when she began to quote the psychologist, he cut her short: 'Can I come over and you can tell me then? Vivienne is away and I've been on my own all day. I could use some company—and perhaps some of your pizza as well!'

He sounded so disconsolate, and Carla had her own memories of lonely city Sundays that never seemed to end, so she agreed.

Revel Braden wouldn't approve, she reflected while she chopped tomatoes, mushrooms, green peppers and black olives, and fried bacon and grated some cheese. Well, she was glad. It was time for an act of defiance. He had occupied her thoughts too frequently in the last six weeks, and it wasn't natural or normal. Nothing in her life could match her present confusion of mind. It was as if Revel possessed her, despite the distance separating them; he mattered, his opinions had become important to her.

That was why a show of independence was necessary, for her own benefit, not Revel's, since she still had no intention of having anything to do with him again. He had no right to dictate to her, while she had every right to choose her own friends. She must bring an end to this haunting power he exerted over her without even being present, or she would never know peace again.

It was some time after nine o'clock when Bernard arrived. They ate at the beautiful kitchen table Carla had found at an auction, and which she had spent many hours stripping and restoring to its original condition. Afterwards, they took their glasses and the remainder of the sharp, young wine they were drinking through to the lounge while the coffee was percolating.

They discussed Justine at length and agreed that Bernard should not be hasty in taking action, remembering that at fourteen, outright banning would inevitably invest the cult with all the irresistible allure of forbidden fruit. Instead, he would attend one of the rallies himself, perhaps investigate the preacher and only then, if he deemed it necessary, decide on how he should wean Justine away.

'And take a look at Marigold's feature when it appears in *Afrinews*,' Carla suggested when, at about half-past eleven, he was leaving. 'She has delved quite deeply into that preacher's background, I think.'

'I might leave it where Justine will see it too. She's an intelligent girl beneath her hang-ups, and she has considerable respect for the media.' Bernard paused, brown eyes wistful, as if her opening of the front door was a dismissal he would have preferred not to receive. 'Thanks for thinking it important enough to contact me, Carla . . . and for listening . . . and for talking.'

'You're my best friend here, Bernard?' She made it a question, suddenly needing the reassurance that that was all he was. Guilt was back with her, and the feeling that she had betrayed something by having him here tonight.

'If that's what you want,' he conceded reluctantly.

'Of course.' Deliberately, she made her tone light.

'I'm glad,' he said heavily, but he smiled and

shrugged. 'Just recently I've had the impression that you . . . were in the process of moving on.'

'Oh, no,' Carla said slowly. 'How could I? How should I?'

It was no answer, but it seemed to satisfy him. He touched her hand and said goodnight, promising to be in touch.

She had just carried their glasses and coffee cups through to the kitchen when the doorbell rang, indicating his return.

Always cautious, she paused with her hand on the door chain, thinking she really should have a peephole installed.

'Bernard? Why have you come back?'

'It's not bloody Bernard, damn you! Let me in, Carla.'

The harsh voice had reverberated through her mind so often in the last six weeks that she recognised it instantly, and her fingers trembled with her excitement as she released the chain and opened the door.

Booted and wearing a black leather jacket above his jeans, Revel strode through the hall and into the lounge. Instantly alert to the vibrant anger emanating from him, Pasht leapt up from her chair and fled in the direction of the kitchen.

'I'm sorry,' Carla began nervously, having followed him after closing the front door. 'I thought you were Bernard returning . . . He was here just a little while ago, you see.'

'I know,' Revel stated savagely as he removed his jacket and flung it on to the chair Pasht had vacated. 'I recognised his car. I've been sitting out there debating the merit of coming in and throwing him out. Luckily for him, he left before I had reached a decision.'

His slanting eyes glittered with barely concealed rage as they rested on her, and Carla could feel herself shaking as she stared back at him.

He looked tired. His face was shadowy, the hollows seemingly deeper, making his bones appear more prominent. His mouth twisted grimly and he needed a shave. Fatigue was straining what control he had over his fury, Carla realised.

It made him as dangerous and unpredictable as a creature of the wild. He was tired, angry, obviously misjudging her again, and she should have been angry in her turn. Instead, all she could think was——

Oh, my darling, my dear love!

CHAPTER FIVE

RELIEF washed through Carla, warm and healing. She felt a floating weightlessness, as if she were buoyed up by elation. There had been nothing abnormal about her obsession with Revel. Instead, it had been the most natural thing in the world, and now she had him back, safe. She need never feel guilty or ashamed again.

But regret—— She lowered her almond-shaped eyes hastily, her face flushing, and her brief euphoria receded as she realised the disaster she had brought on herself. Revel could only destroy her. With nothing of softness in his nature, he had nothing to give her, certainly not the long-term loving she needed, wanted, so achingly already. She doubted if he was capable of that sort of deep caring; all he could offer was passion—angry, contemptuous passion, because he couldn't even see her clearly.

She turned slightly away from him before glancing quickly at his dark cynical face, a shy upward look out of the corners of her eyes, unconsciously provocative, but awareness had made her self-conscious and unable to regard him directly.

'Do ... do you want some coffee?' she ventured tentatively. 'Or wine? And there's some pizza left if you're hungry.'

'The only thing I want is you,' Revel told her harshly.

'Oh.' Disconcerted, she couldn't think of any reply and she felt her colour deepening again. She wanted him too, though not in the same way, but he must never know or he would break her utterly.

He laughed, a bleak, bitter sound that made her wince. 'God! How many kinds of fool does the world contain, I wonder? I learnt long ago that only a fool has faith, but it's another kind of fool who needs to learn the lesson twice over. Do you know, Carla, all through these last six weeks while I've been away, I've kept thinking of you, remembering your words at our last meeting. . . . You said you couldn't and wouldn't lie in the heat of passion. I thought—perhaps it was the truth, perhaps Franck isn't her lover. It became important to me to get back and see you again and ask you one more time about your relationship with him. This time I was going to listen, and look, and gauge for myself whether you were telling the truth, instead of assuming a lie before you had even opened your mouth. It seemed so important to do that, that instead of collecting my Honda and going for my usual burn-out down Chapman's Peak way, I came straight here—to find Franck's car parked outside, and it was well over an hour before he emerged and drove away. Damn you, Carla, damn you to hell. That's the last time I . . . believe, or trust. I should have known better anyway.'

His voice had dropped and was oddly hollow, and Carla was now able to face him directly again, her lips parted and a dawning glow in her eyes. He had wanted to believe, she exulted. That was a start, at least, and she could still persuade him——

She said quickly, breathlessly, 'But you were right to believe, Revel! Bernard wasn't here to . . . I mean, we didn't make love——'

'Tonight?' he interrupted sardonically. 'Can I believe even that? I suppose I can, since you don't look as if you've been made love to just recently——'

Appalled, Carla stared at him. Dear God, how was she to break through such a hard casing of cynicism and make him believe her? It was now desperately important that he should do so, and know her for the woman she was, not the promiscuous marriage-wrecker circumstances had conspired to make her appear. He had wanted to believe her, she reminded herself, so somewhere there, interred beneath all that cynicism, a small core of faith must be still extant, an inclination to trust. . . . But with his usual swift forming of an opinion, he now believed it had been betrayed, and he would only lay it bare to her persuasion with the greatest reluctance.

'Revel, please, won't you . . . won't you sit down and listen to me as you originally intended doing?' she began softly but he didn't move.

'A stupid inclination which misled me. I don't intend it to happen again.' He smiled ironically. 'Blame it on the events I've been covering. It's a common enough syndrome among war correspondents and soldiers alike: home seems sweeter and women kinder and more beautiful than they actually are. In a way it's worse for the journalists than for those doing the fighting, because we're constantly in competition, whereas the troops whether legitimate or guerilla are united by whatever it is they happen to be fighting for. But afterwards, we're all the same, we all want a woman.'

'Any woman,' Carla suggested scathingly, as bitter suspicion assailed her.

Was he being strictly truthful in saying he had come straight here? Vivienne Franck was the woman he loved, but Bernard had said Vivienne was away. Had Revel tried to contact her first?

'Only you, Carla, not just any woman,' Revel was answering her broodingly, and he added quietly, 'Damn you.'

'Revel——'

'Though it would have been better had I taken my customary ride first before coming here,' he went on, ignoring the entreaty in her voice. 'But you're no more a romantic innocent than I am, are you? You're twenty-four and have at least some experience.'

Only, she hadn't, but he didn't know that and

wouldn't believe her or even listen if she tried to tell him in his present mood.

'Come here, Carla,' he commanded harshly, holding out a hand.

She hesitated. She still didn't want him to make love to her like this, despising her and uncaring of her feelings. Then she looked at him, and saw the tortured hunger that made his eyes blaze and twisted his lips into a line of suffering. He needed her! He really needed her, for tonight at least, and if Vivienne or any other woman would have served him as well, she would not think about that. Not now.

With an inarticulate murmur, Carla moved towards him and they came together in a wild embrace as she collapsed into his arms, her head falling back as her lips parted to receive his kiss. The world exploded around them, and they were the cause and the effect, the first contact igniting a raging inferno of desire, the fiery impact of which sent them spinning madly out of control, helpless against the shocking force of their need, the end inevitable and not to be denied.

Any further doubts Carla might have had about what they were doing were dispelled by the urgency of their hunger for each other. Right and wrong were mere concepts, nothing to do with this white-hot reality of passion, and the traditional values instilled by her parents were swamped by the welter of erotic sensation that was overwhelming her so completely.

Revel's mouth on hers was hot and hard, and she responded feverishly, moaning her impatience for more, and taut tremors shook her body as she felt his hands on her, sure and skilled and swift in caressing, arousing. A few minutes previously she had stepped towards him as a martyr, expecting to be used, to be doing all the giving and receiving nothing, but now her desire matched his and was mounting with every second that passed in his arms with his mouth still savage and sensual in exploring the moist softness of hers. Carla felt the need to know him on her, in her, like a searing emptiness, a void he must fill if she was not to lose her mind.

Her shoes, skirt and blouse, as well as Revel's shirt, had all been discarded by the time he lifted her and carried her to her bedroom, seeming to know instinctively which door led to it. The small lamp beside the bed was on, illuminating the prettily demure Laura Ashley fabrics and matching wallpaper, a virgin's room with a single three-foot bed, but Revel was beyond noticing the incongruity of it in comparison with the woman he believed her to be.

He lowered her on to the bed and joined her there, his mouth devouring hers once more, the softness of the duvet beneath them, for they needed no covering. It was a cool night but the heat they were generating was torrid, scorching them, and intensifying all the time.

Though his hands were shaking, Revel was swift in removing her remaining garments, her snowy bra with the broderie anglaise trim and the tiny matching panties, and when he raised himself to look down on what he had revealed, Carla felt no fear, only a loving joy that the sight could give him pleasure, and a deeply feminine pride in knowing that she was perfectly formed, her skin flawless and smooth as satin.

'Oh, God, Carla!' Revel groaned anguishedly. 'I've longed for this, dreamed of this, for so long. . . . These last six weeks. . . . Six long, bloody, aching weeks.'

His voice shook with intensity and she could deceive herself that he meant her alone. His hand touched her swollen breasts, tormenting the hardened puckered nipples, and slid down over her heaving ribcage past her slender waist and over the flatness of her stomach to the soft dark triangle and sweet heart of feminine mystery between her thighs, and Carla shuddered with pleasure, whimpering softly as she drew his dark head down to her aching breasts.

She loved him so much! If only she could say it——
If only he loved her, then she could have done so, and
there would have been no secrets between them because
then he would have been able to believe in her.

Revel's lips and tongue played with her breasts,
stroking, circling and kissing, over and over again until
her nipples were inflamed and tender, and then moved
on, until she sobbed with desire.

'Please, Revel, please!' She didn't know the words,
but her need to have the final mystery revealed to her
was implicit in her ragged, beseeching voice.

Breathing rapidly, his skin as moist as hers, Revel
moved a little away from her to remove the remainder
of his clothes, and Carla's hazel eyes glowed with
wonder and adoration as they rested on his magnificent
body, aggressively masculine and beautiful enough to
close her throat and make tears stand in her eyes. He
was beautiful, so beautiful, and it was awesome and
humbling to know he wanted to submerge his body in
hers.

'I want you so much.' His voice was hoarse, little
more than a whisper, and with aeons-old instinct, Carla
began to explore his body as he had done hers, her
fingers stroking over his taut stomach towards the hard
demanding centre of his maleness, and she exulted in
his sharply indrawn breath and the effect her touch had
on his pulsating loins.

'Carla!' He caught her hands and dragged them
away, pushing her back into the softness of the duvet
and lifting himself over her. 'Carla, I'm sorry, I can't
wait any longer.'

She didn't want him to wait. There was a gathering
heat where she wanted that hard male strength,
intensifying to an unbearably exquisite flame when she
felt the swollen warmth of his manhood surge against
her as she parted her thighs instinctively, arching in
wanton invitation.

Then there was a sharp, piercing agony and Revel's cry of triumph at the moment of possession was mingled with her own shocked cry of pain and protest.

'Oh, my God, no!'

Rigid with rejection, Carla thrashed frenziedly in brief rebellion against the alien male domination she had never known before, the fierce, deepening possession Revel was beyond controlling. It seemed an outrage of scandalous intimacy, a liberty, and tears lay on her cheeks. . . .

Then she saw his white, tormented face and her resentment of his invasion receded along with pain, to be replaced by a rekindled warmth. She flung her arms round him and clung, in a gesture that was part apology, part forgiveness.

It was quickly over and he rolled away from her to lie with his face turned away. After his breathing had returned to normal, he lay so still that Carla thought he had fallen asleep until she noticed the tension that held him rigid beside her. She was shivering now, and she wanted to reach out, to comfort him and be comforted, but her reserve prevented her. He was still a stranger to her. It was ironical. They had just been as close as two people could be, physically, and yet a million miles of space lay betwen them, thick with misunderstanding.

Finally he stirred, moving to sit on the edge of the bed, his tanned back to her and his dark head bent, and the terrible silence continued for a while.

'Why?' he asked eventually in a raw tone as he reached for his underpants and jeans. 'Why did you . . . God, Carla, how could you let me do that to you?'

'I'm sorry,' she murmured awkwardly. 'I should have told you.'

'And I probably wouldn't have believed you,' Revel acknowledged flatly with bleak self-knowledge.

He pulled on his boots before standing up and

turning to regard her, and Carla knew a sense of shock that a face could become so grim and ravaged in so short a space of time. A bitterly antagonistic light flared in his eyes as he appraised her wet face, her bruised mouth and the marks of passion just beginning to show on her body, before he winced visibly and averted his gaze from the further sad evidence that she had been a virgin. Clumsily, Carla pulled up one edge of the duvet to cover her now chilled nakedness, wondering desperately how this situation could be mended now, when so much damage had been done, on both sides.

'I'm sorry,' she began again through chattering teeth.

'I'm sure you are,' Revel concurred savagely as he zipped up his jeans. 'It wasn't what you expected, was it? My God, you've used me nicely. . . .' He paused, apparently looking for his shirt before remembering it was in the lounge. Then, a further upsurge of anger making his eyes blaze, he went on: 'God, Carla, how could you let me do that to you? It shouldn't have been that way, not for your first time. However inexperienced you were, you must have realised I was in no condition to show you any consideration. . . . What were you doing, trying to punish me for believing you and Franck were lovers? Damn you, why did you do it?'

She wanted to say—because I love you and you needed me. But how could she? Seeing his tortured expression, she understood that he was lacerated by some obscure kind of male guilt. Virgins were taboo, and he was perhaps trying to turn the blame away from himself and on to her.

She looked away from him with a shuddering sigh. Typically, she would rather endure his condemnation than add to his guilt by telling him she loved him. To suffer requires less courage than to witness his suffering. To confess the truth would make him blame himself even more bitterly. He would hate himself and start resenting her or worse, feel himself under some sort of obligation to her, and she couldn't bear that. Pity would be even worse than contempt.

A touch of anger added itself to her turbulent emotions. She couldn't tell him she loved him, but by now he ought to have realised it for himself. How else could she have let him possess her?

Bitterly she accused. 'Isn't that a typically male attitude, blaming me for something that required your participation?'

'I wouldn't have taken you if you had been unwilling.'

'Well, I wasn't unwilling, was I?' Carla retorted tartly.

He had to stand at the foot of the bed and she pulled her aching body up against the big continental cushion, feeling at a disadvantage, lying down while he stood there like some dark judge passing sentence.

'How is it that Franck isn't your lover?'

'For pity's sake, Revel, he's married and——'

'So who had the scruples, he or you?' he cut in sardonically.

'You bastard!' Carla was pale, her swollen lips trembling with hurt. Then an odd sort of pride made her eyes brilliant. He had awakened her love, without ever doing anything to merit it—but of course, she couldn't tell him she loved him.

'Well, I don't think it was you,' Revel assured her ruthlessly. 'You used me, and probably you deserved what you got, though I'm sorry I hurt you. But I won't let you play me like that again, Carla. I'm getting out of your life and staying out of it, as I should have had the wit to do in the first place, and I'll be grateful if you'll keep away from me in future.'

'You have my word on that,' she called after him, holding back a threatening flood of tears, as he strode out of the room.

By the time she had dragged herself off the bed,

found her golden velour robe and followed him to the lounge, Revel had his shirt and jacket on again and was on the point of leaving.

He paused, assessing her moodily, and then his mouth curved, but without humour. 'I really should have gone for that ride, shouldn't I?'

'Yes, you should,' Carla concurred in a frosty little voice, wrapping her arms about her body. She was still shivering, and she felt sore and violated, but if only he could have offered her some tenderness now, the merest hint of comfort, nothing else would matter, she knew.

But Revel's face remained hard and hostile, as he added harshly, 'I meant what I said just now, Carla. Stay out of my life, and I'll stay out of yours.'

She nodded, suddenly unable to speak. He was leaving and she would probably never see him again. Desolation added itself to the chill that gripped her. It was like watching her own life-force ebb away to see him go, because he was taking away with him her heart and her only chance of love and happiness, for deep within her lay the knowledge that she would not love another man.

In a frozen state, moving like an automaton, she locked up and fed Pasht before running a bath and lowering her strangely lethargic body into the warm water. The warmth brought a revival of the emotion that had been suspended since Revel's departure, and a wild storm of weeping shook her.

But so much anguish was futile, she reflected bitterly when it was over and she was drying herself. There was no point in it, because there was nothing she could do to mend matters and nothing for her to hope for. All Revel could offer her was both the best and the worst, pity if he should learn of her feelings, and that was something she wouldn't be able to bear.

She pulled on a nightdress and made her way towards her bed. She ought to have been in her darkroom, developing the photos to illustrate Marigold's article, but a deep, weary lassitude impaired her usual professionalism. All she wanted was sleep, and when she woke up she would begin trying to forget the shattering effect of Revel Braden's brief, wounding presence in her life. Just to forget. . . .

But even if she had possessed the strength of mind to deliberately submerge her emotions, she was not destined to forget.

How could you forget a man when he not only possessed your mind and emotions, but had actually left a physical part of himself trapped within your body, another life to grow and remind you constantly of how you had been joined on one devastating night?

Carla suspected she was pregnant very quickly. Pre-menstrual tension was something she kept a careful record of because in addition to making her anti-social and hypersensitive to the slightest hint of criticism, she also believed it made her clumsy and less adept than usual with her cameras, while all the minor accidents in her darkroom occurred at that time.

But this month, the usual weepiness and back-ache failed to assail her and instead of being tense, she felt lazy, lethargically disinclined to do anything but sit dreaming in the sun, and she found herself going to bed earlier than usual in the evenings and reluctant to get up in the mornings.

When she didn't have her period, she went to see the doctor she had been attending ever since that first year in the city when, coming from the healthily dry Karoo, she had seemed to succumb to every virus around before acquiring immunity.

She felt a little embarrassed to be explaining what she suspected, but Dr Basson was patient with her and, after confirming that she was pregnant, he merely said discreetly that if she had problems or doubts she was free to discuss them with him and he would do his best to advise her.

'I haven't really thought about practicalities, but I should be able to manage,' Carla murmured, feeling a little lightheaded and torn betwen pain and a purely feminine sense of triumph that had its roots in an atavistic feeling that she was now a complete woman, fulfilling the purpose for which she had been designed.

'You know you can ask the father for assistance?' Dr Basson probed, but that was a subject she was totally unable to discuss yet and she lowered her eyes, staring at her tense hands as they played restlessly with the fabric of her blue and cream plaid skirt. Seeing she wasn't able to reply, the doctor added, 'You're an adult, Carla, and don't need gratuitous advice from me except on medical matters, but one word of warning, if you don't mind—a man has a right to know that he's going to be a father, even if circumstances prevent his actually being a father in the spiritual and emotional sense. I've seen too much trauma caused by girls and women withholding such information.'

'I ... need to think about it,' Carla muttered awkwardly.

'Of course,' he said and went on to give her practical advice about diet, and information she would be needing later about exercise classes, hospitals and baby clinics since, without her actually saying so, he knew she would be keeping the baby.

A baby! Revel's baby, she reminded herself with a tearful smile as she drove to the fruit and vegetable market behind Golden Acre in the heart of Cape Town. She had been Dr Basson's last patient that Saturday morning and the shops had all closed for the afternoon, but the Coloured stallholders were still there, and it was they whom she wanted.

She was feeling more vulnerable than she had ever done in her life and she needed to be close to people who were kind for a while. She rarely photographed people professionally, but she had a private portfolio to which she added whenever the mood took her, and the stallholders along with the flowersellers were among her favourite subjects.

She forgot it was a damp, grey day when she saw their lined faces, every one with a story. They were the beating heart of the old Mother City, and its character, and she never felt shy with them, because their mocking comments as she photographed them were never unkindly meant. They were kind in an often sarcastic way, infinitely generous, and possessed of that unfailing, bitter humour that had enabled them to rise above the difficulties of the complex mixture of acceptance and rejection that were the fate of those of mixed heritage in a race-obsessed land.

She talked to them while she worked, and their children and grandchildren danced about her and ran up and down, joyously splashing through puddles, but her mind was occupied with the life she now knew was growing inside her, too small to even look like a baby yet, she supposed. There was so long to wait, about eight months, before she could hold her child in her arms and look for likenesses to its father.

She had never felt like this before, swinging wildly between elation and fright. There were so many things to be considered and she didn't know if she could cope.

Remembering her upbringing, she supposed she ought to be feeling a sense of shame, and perhaps she would later, when other people knew. Certainly there was a raw pain in her breast whenever she contemplated her parents' reactions. They were elderly now, and old-fashioned, and they had trusted her to adhere to the principles they had instilled in her. They would be so ashamed, feeling she had let them and herself down, and she didn't know how she would find the courage to tell them and know that she was causing them pain.

They would have to know, though, since she would be keeping the baby, and she couldn't just sever all contact with them. They would be expecting her to visit the farm later that year, by which time her pregnancy would be showing, and she had to find a way of preparing them so that they wouldn't receive too much of a shock.

Deciding she had enough photos, Carla slung her cameras over one shoulder and accepted the big, shiny green apple one of the stallholders was offering her, said goodbye and made her way slowly back to where she had parked the Renault.

The day was growing darker along with her thoughts, and she sat in the car, eating her apple, while tears kept filling her eyes. She supposed she had made a mess of her life. Twenty-four-year-old women were supposed to be able to take care of themselves. It was sixteen-year-old schoolgirls who got pregnant the first time they went to bed with a man, and here she was, joining their number. God, Marigold would find it hilarious.

There was so much to be decided, and the future had become a frightening prospect. She had no idea how much it cost to bring up a child, though she had an idea that it was after they started school that they became expensive. But she would have to carry on working, so there would be crèche fees to pay, since she could hardly leave a baby to the care of a neighbour as she could Pasht. She must save as much as she could during the next few months, she decided. Fortunately the university would have no objection to her going on working right through—a lecturer had thrilled her students by going into labour in their midst only last year—and she had few fears that her photography would prove too much for her although she might have to stop dangling from half-constructed bridges after a while. About her position at *Afrinews*, she was less certain. Nathaniel Nash was notoriously straitlaced and would tolerate no hint of promiscuity in most of his employees although he was hypocritical enough to turn a blind eye to the lifestyles of such star journalists as Revel Braden, but surely the Old Man's views must have become a bit modernised; he read his own newspapers and must know that the values to which he adhered were unique and beyond the reach of most people.

Carla smiled faintly. Anyway, with all the illicit affairs and other irregular activities the *Afrinews* editor and staff took such delight in concealing from the Old Man, she could probably count on their co-operation in her own case, and as long as she kept on producing satisfactory photos there was no need for her to have anything to do with Mr Nash, so he need never know—and if not, she was good enough to get a job with any other newspaper group or to make a living from freelancing.

Her thoughts swung to Revel as she started the car, and she realised she had been avoiding thinking about him and his part in the matter. Now Dr Basson's words kept echoing in her mind—a man had a right to know he was going to be a father. She knew it was true. She owed it to both Revel and herself, but she was afraid. Considering the way he despised her, and his inability to trust, he was sure to think she was trying to impose on him in some way, trap him into marriage or extract money from him, and she didn't think she could bear any more of his contempt.

But he had a right to know. . . .

The dilemma exercised her mind for the remainder of the weekend, making her restless and distressed, and when she went into the *Afrinews* offices on the Monday morning she looked wan and weary, dark circles beneath her eyes standing out against the pallor of her face, but by now she had made her decision. She would let Revel know, but make it clear that she expected nothing from him.

Only, she was going to do it by telephone. She knew she was a coward, but she just couldn't face him again. That was why she had come in to *Afrinews*, to find out if he was in Cape Town just now and what his home telephone number was.

She waited until after nine o'clock that night, by which time she was feeling sick and panicky. Her hands shook so badly that she was in danger of getting a wrong number, so she put the receiver down and drew several shaky breaths before trying again. Almost, she hoped there would be no reply. He could be out. She had learnt that morning that he had just returned two days ago from an Asian country where some election results had sparked off appalling violence, so he could be making the most of this time at home. He could be with Vivienne Franck who was, after all, the woman he loved—as much as he was capable of loving.

'Braden. Yes?'

Carla swallowed convulsively, wondering if she was going to faint. 'Revel?' she began in a frightened little voice.

'Who is it?' He sounded impatient and she could hear music in the background, romantic mood music, so perhaps Vivienne was there with him.

'It's Carla . . . Carla Duminy,' she said, and her voice sounded husky and disgustingly humble. God, it was ironical, needing to identify herself like this to a man whose body had moved in hers and whose child now rested in her womb. Telling him her surname! She felt cheap——

'Damn it, Carla, I told you to get out of my life,' Revel exploded violently and she winced at the hatred in his voice. 'Get out and stay out. If you want to experiment further, find some other bloody fool to do it with. I won't be used like that again.'

She felt as if her love died in that moment. 'Weren't you using me as well, Revel?' she asked icily. 'All right,

I won't contact you again. I'm sorry I did so tonight, but I suppose I'm like you ... I need to have my lessons repeated.'

She slammed down the receiver and then collapsed on the sofa, weeping bitterly. His cruelty had stunned her, shocked her into facing the reality of what she had done, and for the first time she saw clearly how she had degraded herself. Ah, God, how could she have loved a man who was so brutally cynical? To have let him see her as he had done, when he despised her. He had always made his lack of regard for her callously evident, yet she had gone ahead as if she really was as worthless as he believed, ignoring the value she had always placed on herself. He hadn't deserved her. . . .

She realised that subconsciously she must have been relying on Revel to share this burden with her. Now at last she knew better. She could depend on no one but herself.

She was all alone.

CHAPTER SIX

DURING the next few weeks Carla knew that Revel was out of the country once more, so she was able to relax in the knowledge that there was no danger of encountering him when she went in to *Afrinews*. Nevertheless, she was thinking seriously of resigning because she wouldn't always be able to rely on his absence, since his routine was no routine at all; he came and went as the need arose, flying towards trouble, leaving when it died down—and she had no wish to see him again, ever.

Her feelings these days were ambivalent. She knew now that her love hadn't really died, but it had become shot through with a deep, intense hatred of Revel personally, and resentment of men generally for the way they used women and then refused to admit that they had done so, all masters at turning the blame around and directing it back at her sex.

She knew she was becoming bitter, but she couldn't seem to help it. Too much had hurt her in too short a space of time for her to have been able to adapt philosophically. She was like a person suffering from shock, her equilibrium savagely disturbed, and she often found herself crying as she worked or at the wheel of her car as she sank deeper and deeper into a black abyss of depression, worse by far than the daemons of PMT, because now she was actively suffering.

Occasionally, panic dragged her up into the light again, and she would make an effort to organise herself and her future. She still hadn't found the courage to inform her parents. The cowardly idea of contacting her sister-in-law and asking her to do it for her was soon dismissed. She couldn't burden Linda with such a task. This was her problem, and hers alone. Not even Revel, half its cause, shared it.

A baby—a problem! When she loved babies. She loved this one, but the unhappiness surrounding its conception prevented her from feeling much pride or pleasure in the prospect of its birth as yet.

Pregnancy itself wasn't too difficult. It didn't show yet; if anything, she looked thinner, although she forced herself to eat for the baby's sake and took long walks along various Cape beaches, and if she was permanently exhausted, it had less to do with pregnancy itself than with sleepless nights during which she lay tortured in the dark, worrying and remembering, always remembering. . . .

One bonus was that she felt the cold less than in previous winters, and as for the morning sickness she had confidently expected, she decided it was misnamed. She was occasionally sick at other times of the day, certainly, but never first thing in the morning.

She was living very quietly. Her lifestyle had never been riotous, and now she saw very few people when she was not working. She had lunch with Bernard a couple of times, and they talked mostly about Justine who had been as shocked as many other people by Marigold Vibor's exposé of the prosperity cults and now stayed at home on Sundays or went sailing with her father.

'Now she's dieting, so I suppose my next worry will be anorexia,' Bernard said resignedly. 'You're looking very . . . slim yourself these days, Carla.'

Not for much longer, she thought sardonically, murmuring something noncommittal about working hard.

In the evenings, she was alone or she saw Mrs Du Plessis, her widowed neighbour, and Marigold occasionally shared her supper if she wasn't covering a story or invited her to exotic little dinners at which she continued to introduce a series of men whom she thought Carla might like.

As yet, Carla had told no one she was pregnant, and she was dreading the day when Marigold must know—Marigold who talked a lot about the population explosion and was very scathing about unplanned babies.

In fact, Marigold possessed all the powers of observation that made a good reporter, and she drew her own conclusions one morning when Carla had been in to see Alastair Carmichael and then stopped at her desk to talk for a while.

A cloud of smoke from Marigold's inevitable cigarette, in a jade holder today, drifted across Carla's face and she felt nausea rising within her. With a muttered excuse, she clapped her hand over her mouth and ran from the office, reaching the cloakroom near the lifts just in time.

She felt weak and shaky when she emerged a few minutes later to find Marigold strolling down the corridor towards her, hands thrust into the pockets of her baggy clown pants, her pansy-coloured eyes thoughtful.

'You okay? You know, Carla, I sometimes think you still need your mother.' She paused to nod curtly to someone emerging from the lifts behind Carla before continuing. 'Forgive me if I'm insulting your intelligence, but is it possible that you're overdue with the curse? You also had to dive for the loo when I lit up the other night, I remember. Plus, you always used to drink coffee and strong Indian tea whereas now you can only face Earl Grey.'

'Yes, I know . . . I mean, I realise.' Taken by surprise, she was stammering. 'You're right. I am. . . . No!'

The last word emerged as a moan of anguish as the person coming from the lifts halted beside them and she saw who it was. She had gone so white that Marigold gripped her arm and Revel put out a hand too, then withdrew it on seeing her look of appalled rejection.

'This is woman-talk, Braden,' Marigold advised sharply.

'I think it's talk that concerns me.' Bitter rage was replacing his shock, and Carla thought she would faint when he looked at her. 'Come with me, Carla. Now! We have to talk about this.'

'No!' She shrank away from him, her protest an agonised whisper. 'There's nothing to talk about. Go away. . . . Leave me alone, Revel, just leave me alone!'

'I wish to God I could!' he muttered with such violent sincerity that she felt as if he had stabbed her.

'Well, make a start now,' Marigold instructed. 'It's what she wants.'

'For God's sake, this has to be discussed, it's my responsibility.' He was talking to Marigold now, not Carla, and he added more quietly, 'I'll take care of her.'

Marigold looked at Carla. 'I think you should go with him, Carla. If I'm reading this situation correctly, he owes you something.' She looked at that taut, impatient face of the man. 'You bastard, Braden.'

'I don't need you to tell me that, Vibor,' he snapped sardonically. 'It's something Carla keeps on proving to me over and over again. Come on, Carla, let's get out of here.'

He had her arm in a relentless grip and she felt too sick and shattered to resist, allowing him to walk her to the lifts.

She leaned against the side of the lift, wondering if she was going to be sick again, but gradually the feeling faded, as did some of her fear, to be replaced by a growing anger against him.

They emerged in the basement parking area and Revel took her arm again, marching her towards his Lamborghini.

'This isn't necessary, Revel, we have nothing to discuss. My car is over there, so let me go, please,' she begged tautly. 'I don't want ... I can manage on my own. It has nothing to do with you.'

'It has everything to do with me,' Revel contradicted her harshly. 'Get in. I'll bring you back to collect your car after we've talked.'

Wearily, she obeyed. She might as well conserve her strength. She had a feeling she would need it presently.

'Where are your cameras?' he asked curtly as they drove out into the busy street.

'I only have a lecture this afternoon,' she explained stiffly. 'Where are we going?'

'God! I don't know, somewhere ... anywhere!'

She remained silent beside him, wishing she could achieve some sort of numbness, some release from the rawness of her feelings, but she had only to glance at Revel to know a tumultuous disturbance of her senses and a throbbing ache in her heart. He looked darker than ever, and generally leaner and harder, while there was something shockingly harsh about the line of his mouth.

Surreptitiously, she undid the button fastening the waistband of her jeans and pulled her chenille sweater lower to conceal it, realising that her waist must be starting to thicken at last. Her anger had had a fragmented quality, but now it was coming together into a compact core, a tight hard knot of concentrated rage.

For once, she would be proof against the devastating power he had over her. A wave of fiercely protective love for her embryo child swept through her, the first truly deep maternal feeling she had experienced since realising she was pregnant. It was her baby; she wanted it desperately, even if he didn't, and she wasn't going to let her child be harmed.

Somewhat to her surprise, she found that Revel was

making for Rhodes Memorial, and then, still the
desert's daughter, she felt relieved. Out in the open, she
wouldn't feel hemmed in, overwhelmed.

He parked in the open carpark beside the memorial,
got out and walked to the expanse of green grass that
sloped upwards to where the trees began. Carla sat still
for a moment, then, leaving her bag in the car, she
followed him.

A pale but radiant sun was shining, but the cold wind
that had swept the clouds away was still blowing. Arum
lilies studded the grass and the tame buck moved about
indolently. As it was a weekday morning, only a few
people were about, a handful of young mothers, White
and Coloured, playing or picnicking with their pre-
school children, and one Moslem family in their
traditional concealing garb.

It was a tranquil scene, devoid of harshness, and
normally Carla would have found it soothing, but she
was too aware of Revel, some way up the slope, waiting
for her to catch up with him. She could feel his gaze,
like a laser, examining her, noting that her smooth
shiny hair was longer but still beautifully shaped,
framing a face that was pale and sensitive, faint
shadows lying beneath her suffering eyes, her mouth
vulnerable. And perhaps he was looking for changes in
her figure too, she reflected with some self-conscious-
ness, although he was unlikely to find any. He didn't
know her well enough and, any way, her soft chenille
sweater, in cream and two shades of blue, was
concealing, with batwing sleeves and fairly loose about
her body.

She stopped a little distance from him and looked up
at him, anxiously wondering if he expected her to speak
first, since he continued to watch her in silence. It was a
long look that they exchanged, wary and strained, more
alien to each other than they had ever previously been,
but even hating him, Carla felt the quickening of desire,

a warm ache in her stomach. He was tall and lithe, and the suede jacket open over a thin shirt and the wind in his dark hair gave him a casually virile look.

Oh, God, she wanted him and loved him and hated him.

Finally, Revel said flatly, 'You're pregnant.'

She swallowed painfully. 'Yes.'

'Have you seen a doctor, had it confirmed?'

'Yes.'

'Is it my child, Carla?'

She drew a quick, sharp breath, as if he had slapped her, and her face turned white. Then her eyes went brilliant with rare, uncontrollable temper and she found there was no longer any need to grope for words—they came spilling out of her at a furious rate.

'My God, you swine! After all you've done to me— misjudging me, refusing to listen to me, persecuting me, impregnating me. . . .' She did pause then, because that last sounded so ugly, a betrayal of the child she already loved, but she needed to hit out at Revel and hurt him as he had hurt her so often, and she swept on, 'Making me afraid to tell you and terrified of facing my parents because they'll be so disappointed. . . . You've done all that to me, damn you, you've ruined my life, and then you can still stand there and insult me by implying that it might not be your child that I'm carrying. I hate you, Revel, I really hate you. I think I'd like to see you dead, or better, alive and suffering, really suffering as you've made me suffer——'

'I'm sorry, Carla, but I had to be sure,' Revel cut in heavily but she was still too angry to be surprised by his reluctant apology.

'Sure of what?' she taunted bitterly. 'Sure that I didn't run straight off to some other man after you'd . . . after . . . God! It wasn't such a great experience for me that I had any wish to repeat it. In a million years' time would be too soon.'

He winced and she was glad. He said abruptly, 'I've already apologised.'

'You'll never be sure of anything,' she rushed on heedlessly, and now there was a pain, dull and heavy, like a stone resting in her breast. 'You'll never be able to believe in anyone ordinary and ... and normal, because you deal too much with the cynical, the violent ... unnatural people! You just can't believe there are ordinary people, living ordinary lives, untouched by cynicism—like those women over there and their children. But I'm one of them, Revel, though you'll never understand that. You've thrown away your right to enter and enjoy our sort of world——'

Revel interrupted impatiently, hostility blazing in his eyes as he looked at her. 'We're here to discuss the fact that you're pregnant. So! What are we going to do about it?'

Carla folded her arms about her body, but not because she was cold. It was an instinctive gesture of protection for the tiny life within her. 'We aren't going to do anything,' she stated pointedly. 'This doesn't concern you, Revel, your part in the matter is over, you had your pleasure, and I'll be the one to pay for it. I'll handle this on my own.'

He looked at her rather strangely, a long thoughtful look, and she realised with fresh anguish that he no longer even desired her as he had once. Where he was concerned, once had definitely been enough, because for him there were always other women, Vivienne Franck, Noelle Malherbe. . . .

'I want you to marry me,' Revel was saying quietly.

For a few seconds Carla could only stare at him. Then a brittle laugh escaped her.

'Congratulations, Revel, that must be one of the first self-sacrificing impulses of your life. Luckily for you, I'm not taking you up on it,' she added mockingly. 'You've made it very clear that you don't want me in your life, on more than one occasion, so I can imagine how quickly you'd start regretting it.'

'I . . . Oh, my God!' He had paled beneath his tan and his voice was hoarse and urgent as he went on, 'Carla, was this what you telephoned me about, to tell me . . . ah, hell! I should have guessed! It just never entered my mind until I heard you and Vibor talking this morning.' He smiled without humour.

Carla flushed. 'Well, anyway——'

'Well, anyway, we're going to get married,' he supplied forcefully.

'No.' She pressed the tips of her fingers to the centre of her brow where she could feel the beginnings of a tension headache. 'This is my child, Revel, and I'll decide its future. I don't need you.'

'It's my child as well, and I have the right——'

'You have no rights. Yes, biologically you helped to create it, but I'm the mother and most of the rights are mine. I'm the one who has to carry it for months, and get fat and breathless and clumsy and give birth to it and feed it. So don't tell me you have rights.'

'Think of our child's rights, Carla. He has a right to know that his parents at least tried to give him the background of a united family. . . . If the marriage doesn't work out, he'll at least know we cared enough to try. It's the endeavour that counts, not its success or failure.'

'He!' Carla's voice had an edge of hysteria now. 'Listen to you, the typical arrogant male, assuming you've made a son. What happens when it turns out to be a daughter?'

'Oh, for pity's sake,' Revel said impatiently. 'I was talking . . . colloquially, if you like. The same applies to a daughter.'

'I still won't marry you, Revel,' she declared tensely. 'What sort of example will it be for a child, a marriage without love, a forced marriage?'

'Most marriages end up loveless, however they begin,' Revel claimed cynically. His hands fastened on her shoulders, fingers digging mercilessly into her as control slipped from him and his eyes glazed with hatred. 'Damn it, Carla, you talk about your rights, but don't you owe me something, some say in the future of the child I've helped to create? You think of yourself as the injured party, but you've wronged me just as surely. You let me make love to you and conceived my child, and now you attempt to deny me——'

'Of course, you were reluctant and I seduced you?' Carla cut in scathingly with a revival of anger.

'I'd have been reluctant as hell, had I known you were a virgin.'

'And you admitted that you wouldn't have believed me if I'd tried to tell you,' she reminded him acidly. 'So stop blaming me, Revel ... and stop concerning yourself with this. Who knows, perhaps I'll have a miscarriage!' she concluded flippantly.

He took his hands away from her shoulders and looked at her with silent disgust for a few moments. Then he drew a breath as if regaining his self-control, and said quietly, 'Let's both stop apportioning blame, Carla. It's done and can't be undone. We have this baby to consider now. Look at it rationally. Marriage will make things easier for you too. For instance, telling your parents will be much less difficult if you can explain first that you're married.'

Suddenly Carla felt weak and weary, drained of all will. It would be a relief to share her burden, let him take some of the responsibility, and perhaps she did owe it to her child to at least start its life in conventional fashion, however the marriage ended up— and she couldn't see it lasting.

She looked at Revel, her hazel eyes blank and empty.

'All right,' she said flatly. 'I'll marry you.'

Then she turned and walked away down the slope.

She was sitting in the car when he joined her, her hands lying loose and unoccupied in her lap, a curiously defenceless attitude.

'As soon as possible, I think?' Revel queried expressionlessly.

'Yes.'

'I'll arrange it if you'll let me have your identity documents.'

'Yes. I . . . I'd like to be married in a church please. Not a proper wedding or anything, but one of the established Churches.'

Otherwise she couldn't feel properly married and quite suddenly it seemed vitally important that she should do so. It would be a flimsy enough marriage as it was, and needed all the solidity she could inject into it.

'As you wish.' Revel sounded cold. 'Do you want your parents present?'

'No . . . no, I don't think so.' She shook her head doubtfully, trying to think clearly. 'I'm twenty-four and if I explain that it's a sudden thing, they'll understand. . . . We'll have to see them later, though. I think I'll only tell them that we're married to start with, and later on I can tell them I'm going to have a baby and . . . and when it is born they can draw their own conclusions.'

'Is there anyone you want to attend our . . . wedding, then?'

'Marigold, perhaps, and Mrs Du Plessis, my neighbour,' she ventured vaguely. 'I can't think of anyone else.'

'Not Bernard Franck?' Revel taunted.

'No!' It would mean inviting Vivienne and she didn't want Revel's mistress present at her marriage to him.

'Not?' he drawled. 'Come! If he has been too . . . honourable to make love to you, he's surely capable of wearing a brave face to see you married to another man.'

'Shut up!' Carla said fiercely, and he laughed softly.

Realisation of the enormity of what she was doing was beginning to impinge on her now, and she felt apprehensive about the future. God knew what sort of marriage theirs would be, with so much mistrust and resentment on Revel's part. He would feel trapped and it was clear that he resented her for being pregnant. She suspected that he also felt some guilt regarding her, although he was trying to bury it by blaming her, and ultimately that could only add to his resentment.

She didn't even know what sort of marriage he intended it to be and, now that her anger had abated, she was too inhibited to ask. If he no longer found her desirable, would he expect to have other women— Vivienne? She didn't think she could bear that. However discreet he was, her pride would revolt.

She sighed softly, drawing a sharp glance from Revel. If only she possessed the qualities necessary to hold a man's interest, but she lacked them all, great beauty, dazzling wit and experience. He had made love to her once and that had satisfied what had once been a raging hunger in him. In her, it still burnt, more fiercely than ever, because she loved him in a dark tortured way and yearned to know his possession without the pain and shock that had attended her first experience of it.

A sob rose in her throat but she stifled it. If Revel wanted to make love to her when they were married, she wouldn't resist him. Perhaps, with a little more experience, she would learn to satisfy him so that he didn't need other women. She might as well try, anyway; surely she couldn't be hurt any more than she had been already. . . .

She would have to learn not to crave his love, though, she cautioned herself, and blushed at her thoughts. Where was her pride? It was humiliating, degrading, to be so besotted that she was content to settle for lust and do without love.

She deserved more, and how long would it be before she reached the absolute nadir of begging for his love? He was going to feel trapped as it was, saddled with a wife and child he didn't want.

A man of his temperament and following the career he did shouldn't really marry even if he loved, and she must be careful not to cling, and never, ever, to let him guess she loved him—unless, of course, a miracle happened and he learnt to love her.

And what a miracle that would be, Carla reflected hollowly, when whatever love he was even capable of was given to Vivienne Franck? Oh, was ever a more fragile marriage contracted, flawed in every department? Marriage—it would be more like a minefield. It took place two weeks later in a small Anglican church and for Carla it proved an uncomfortably nerve-racking occasion. There was something terribly ironical about hearing Revel make promises he probably had little intention of keeping, in that remote, hard voice, and she almost wished she hadn't requested a church ceremony since it seemed like blasphemy. Her own vows were sincere, but made with a shy stammer. Revel's ritual kiss afterwards did nothing to reassure her, his lips cool and firm in the brief contact they made with the trembling softness of hers.

She didn't feel bridal at all in her soft cream two-piece outfit, sprigged with tiny sprays of wine and lilac flowers, the fitted jacket having a small peplum which flattered her still slender waist.

Afterwards they went with their guests to a luxurious hotel —'We'll have to provide a reception of some sort. It's only the prospect of free drink afterwards that makes weddings bearable for most people,' Revel had claimed cynically.

'Just as well you didn't invite old Nat Nash or you'd have had to have a dry reception,' Alastair Carmichael confirmed, eschewing the champagne provided by the hotel in favour of neat Scotch.

Revel had invited him and his wife, along with *The Courant's* editor and his, plus another journalist, while Carla's only guests were Mrs Du Plessis and Marigold.

Carla looked round at them and realised that Mrs Du Plessis and the two editors' wives were probably the only people who accepted this marriage at face value. Alastair and the man from *The Courant* seemed somewhat perplexed even now, probably because they knew Revel was not basically a marrying man, while Marigold was frankly disapproving, glowering at everyone, lighting a succession of cigarettes and hastily stubbing them out when she remembered they made Carla feel sick—rather pointlessly, since the other journalist was smoking, but she was at least tactful enough not to mention that they had a pregnant woman in their midst.

'Are you sure you know what you're doing?' she demanded of Carla in an undertone when they were free of everyone's attention for a moment.

Carla's smile was wry. 'It's a bit late to be asking me now.'

'I've been asking you for the last two weeks.' Marigold eyed Revel meditatively. 'Hell, Carla, look at him, that wild and reckless look. He's all right for an affair in fact I guess he's devastating, but as a husband! Candidly, I'd rather be a single parent than take that one on. He's a difficult swine, mean and moody—How can you hope to tame him?'

'I don't think I want to ... tame him,' Carla murmured, flushing.

She was even more embarrassed when Revel's editor said to her, 'Rev tells me you're going down to his cottage at the Point for your honeymoon, so this is my real wedding present to you—the promise of five days of perfect peace, no interruptions at all.'

He then went on to add so many provisional clauses that it seemed likely that their honeymoon wouldn't even begin.

A honeymoon. Carla looked at her gold wedding ring with a feeling of panic. She still didn't know what sort of marriage Revel intended it to be. They had been like polite strangers on the occasions they had met in the last fortnight, and she had been too inhibited to raise the question.

He had simply told her that they would go to this cottage for a few days and she had agreed, as she had agreed to everything else. His servants, Basheer and Ramira Malgas, had spent the previous day at the cottage, cleaning, airing, switching on the refrigerator and stocking it. Mrs Du Plessis was going to look after Pasht while they were away, and Carla would collect her on their return and introduce her to her new home, Revel's house in Rondebosch, and she would give notice to her landlord and arrange the transfer of her belongings, either to his house or, as far as her furniture was concerned, to storage until she had decided what to do with it. She would probably want it when their marriage broke up, Carla speculated with a cynicism she seemed to have caught from Revel.

She sat silent and tense beside him as they began the drive to the Point in the gathering dark of a clammy winter's evening, and Revel asked, 'Are you feeling all right?'

'Yes, thank you,' she responded stiltedly.

'You drank far too much champagne for a pregnant woman, but I didn't want to embarrass you by referring to it.'

'Well, thank you.' He had sounded so contemptuous that she felt a prickly need to hit back. 'But perhaps it would be as well if something did go wrong. Then we could end this farce the sooner.'

'We've only been married a few hours and already you're talking about divorce.'

'And aren't you thinking about it?'

He disdained to retaliate, changing the subject quite deliberately. 'Did you telephone your parents this morning?'

'Yes. They were ... surprised, but they wished us luck and said we must visit the farm soon. I gave them the impression that it was ... well, a whirlwind romance. I hope you don't mind?' she added anxiously.

'Why should I? You're the one affected by their opinion, not me,' Revel dismissed her query. 'And Franck? Have you told him?'

'Yes.'

That had been painful and once again she had used that coward's instrument, the telephone. Bernard had been shocked and, she suspected, saddened, but he was too polite to probe, too reserved to protest.

'And?'

'And nothing,' she retorted indifferently.

She wondered why Revel remained so taunting in his references to Bernard, now that he knew they had never been lovers. He seemed to dislike him intensely. Sudden cold seeped through Carla. Was it possible that Revel was jealous of Bernard because of Vivienne? Vivienne loved him, but Bernard was the acknowledged man in her life, whose name and home she shared; Revel was the clandestine lover ... Carla shut her eyes as a wave of agony washed over her. How had Revel told Vivienne of this marriage? Had he told her the truth and assured her that it would make no difference to their relationship?

The awareness that Revel was asking her something dragged her up out of her anguished reverie. 'I'm sorry?' she enquired politely, but with a trace of lingering pain.

'I asked if you and Bernard——' Revel broke off. 'Forget it. Do you want to go on working?'

'Yes. Yes, I think so, for as long as I can, anyway. Lecturing should present no difficulties, and I'll see how my photography goes, perhaps only take the less physically demanding jobs.'

'It will be just as well if you keep busy,' Revel agreed. 'I'll be away a lot of the time. I suppose you've realised that?'

'Yes.'

'Was that what made the prospect of this marriage ... bearable?' he wondered sardonically. 'The knowledge that our partings will be long and frequent?'

'No! Yes. . . . Well, you have to admit that it will be better ... easier, if we don't see too much of each other,' she ventured awkwardly, still inhibited when it came to personal matters.

'For whom?' he derided in a hard voice, with an underlying note of savagery that disturbed her. 'Make no mistake, Carla, on the occasions when I am at home, I shall expect you to be a proper wife to me.'

She needed him to be more explicit, but she was too shy to request it, and by the time they arrived at his cottage in its wild garden above the low ragged cliffs that dropped to the stormy ocean, she still had no idea what sort of marriage Revel wanted.

CHAPTER SEVEN

IN contrast to the exterior, the inside of Revel's cottage was warm and comfortable, furnished with beautiful woods and natural fabrics, the colours restful without being cold, and the floors were strewn with thick, deep rugs in subtly glowing shades that echoed the colours of nature.

But Carla was unable to relax. A combination of nervous tension and her natural reserve reduced her to almost total silence and not even the irritable glances she drew from Revel could make her break out of it. She had created a space about herself, contained within invisible barriers, which she knew probably gave her a misleading air of remote hauteur, but she didn't care, if it deterred any approach Revel might make. She just wasn't ready to handle this situation yet; she wasn't ready for marriage.

Their meal was a silent affair, the tension mounting between them. She had heated one of the meals Ramira Malgas had prepared, and Revel opened a bottle of wine, but Carla declined even a glass, mindful of the champagne she had consumed earlier, although she could have used a little artificially induced courage.

Afterwards, Revel drank coffee and flipped through the English and Afrikaans newspapers he had purchased in Cape Town, and Carla sat still and contained in a comfortable chair, sipping the weak tea she had made for herself because she still couldn't face coffee.

It was an attractive room, designed for relaxation, with shelves of books and records, but Revel's presence was oppressing her and as soon as she had finished her tea, she stood up.

'I think I'll bath and go to bed now if you don't mind,' she said formally, and he nodded indifferently, engrossed in *The Courant*'s leader.

She hesitated, wondering if it was appropriate to say goodnight—or would she be seeing him later? She already knew they would be sharing a bed. The cottage contained two bedrooms and Revel had taken her small suitcase along with his into the larger where a double bed dominated the room. Carla had peeped into the other to discover that it was used as a store-room, the single bed littered with loose papers, box files and two old portable typewriters.

She bathed quickly in the attractive golden-tiled bathroom, self-consciously avoiding the reflection of her naked body in the vast mirror that covered one wall and hastily donning her nightdress and robe. In the bedroom she sat down at the dressing-table and stared at her image with a sinking heart. Without make-up, she looked—plain, she thought, ignoring the exotic mysteriousness of her almond-shaped eyes and the generous softness of her naturally flushed mouth. This new robe she had bought, rich garnet velour, made her look pale, she thought despairingly, although her creamy skin was flawless and she had noticed a sort of translucence lately and wondered if it had anything to do with her pregnancy.

She was brushing her silky brown hair when Revel strolled into the room. Ignoring her completely, he extracted a jade towelling robe from the wardrobe and went into the bathroom, closing the door softly. Carla put down her brush and sat very still.

Oh, God, help me, she thought desperately.

She stood up, looking at the bed and rejecting it. It would look too—inviting, if Revel came back and found her there. There was a bookshelf in the room and she ran her eyes over the collection it contained, finding a novel she had been meaning to read for a long time.

Extracting it, she sat down in the chair beside the bookshelf.

Her eyes were still fastened resolutely to the first page when Revel returned, because she had spent the time while he was showering in imaginings—oh, in imaginings that bordered on the pornographic, she had thought, shamed colour staining her cheeks.

She didn't look up until she became aware that Revel was standing directly in front of her. Then she did, and her heart skipped a beat. He had shaved and his dark hair was still damp and untidy from the shower, his short robe belted loosely, and she knew he wore nothing beneath it. Panic rose in her. It was all too intimate, she wasn't ready——

'What have you found to read?' He took the thick book from her unresisting hands and began to laugh when he saw the title. '*War and Peace*. Ah, no, Carla, it's a worthy ambition but I'm afraid you won't have time to get through that in five days. I have other plans for you. Perhaps I'll allow you to read a word a day like Schulz's Snoopy!'

He tossed the book on to the top of the bookshelf and took her hands, drawing her to her feet. Carla had started to tremble, swaying a little towards him as she felt the familiar weakness in the pit of her stomach, but her eyes remained afraid, and Revel's own narrowed as he noticed.

'You did know I intended this to be a proper marriage, didn't you?'

'I wasn't sure,' she whispered.

Something occurred to him, making him frown. 'I suppose it is safe to make love to you in your condition?'

'Yes. I . . . I asked Dr Basson yesterday and he said yes.' And she had been blushing as much then as she was now.

'I suppose you wish the answer had been no.' As if

antagonised by her hesitancy, Revel sounded suddenly harsh. 'For God's sake, stop looking as if you're going to your own execution. We're here with only each other's company for five days and we might as well pass the time in as pleasant a way as possible.'

Carla lifted her hands to his chest to push him away. She had thought she would be able to let him make love to her, but now she knew she couldn't. Casual desire was not enough. It was too degrading. She wanted his love as well, or nothing. She should never have married him—

'Pleasant?' she enquired in a sceptical, distant little voice.

'Oh, for God's sake, Carla, it won't be like last time, I can promise you that,' Revel said, his hands moving to unfasten the belt of her robe and then sliding inside it, burning through the soft fabric of her white nightdress. 'There won't be pain this time, and I'll make it good for you.'

'No!' She pushed harder against his chest and his robe gaped, bringing her fingers into disturbing contact with the crisp dark hair that curled over his chest. 'I don't . . . I don't want to make love, Revel.'

'But you're going to, sweet,' he drawled. 'I've always thought martyrs were fools, and I've no intention of being one. We've trapped each other neatly, if reluctantly, and I for one intend to derive something positive from the whole sorry situation.'

'Revel, please——' Carla gulped. The play of his hands on her hips, waist and back was inducing a shivering delight.

'I've paid a high price for what I did to you, Carla,' he went on brutally. 'I've given you my name, and I want some return.'

'But you don't even want me any more!'

'Do you think that? You're wrong.' He pulled her closer against him in a violent movement and dropped his mouth to the brightness of hers, kissing her with devastating intensity, almost savage, and her senses reeled as her hands crept up to his shoulders and clung. When he raised his head eventually, the glitter in his eyes matched that in hers. 'I want you, Carla. . . . It has been self-inflicted torture, keeping my hands off you when we've met these last two weeks! I don't know what it is about you, but I could go mad, wanting you . . . wanting to break through all that reserve and quiet hostility and make you want me as much as I do you— want me so that it hurts and you can think of nothing else.'

There was a raw edge to his voice and she stared at him, seeing the mask he had worn recently stripped away. His mouth was turned back as if he were in agony and the light in his eyes was that of a wholly primitive passion, beyond reason and beyond control.

He wanted her, but it was still not enough. Humiliated colour stung her cheeks. If anything it was worse than his no longer desiring her.

'Well, I don't want you,' she lied huskily, her body excitingly aware of the hardness of his.

'You wanted me before and I can make you want me again.'

'No!'

'But yes!' His hands were sliding the robe from her shoulders and it fell to the floor.

'I hate you!' she cried wildly as he pulled her into his arms once more, and in that moment it was the truth. She hated him for the hard intent look in his eyes and the inexorable way in which he was moulding her to him and making her aware of him.

'I think I hate you too, Carla,' he retorted harshly. 'But I still want you. Damn you, you're driving me insane!'

Another long, ruthless kiss captured her, and she fought against herself as much as him, twisting and turning frantically against him, acutely aware of the hard male need her struggles were arousing as she heard her nightdress tear.

'You're so beautiful,' he muttered huskily.

'My body is, you mean!'

'Unbelievably beautiful.'

She could feel his eyes on her slender thighs and still flat stomach and full swollen breasts where the delicate blue veins were visible through the creamy skin. Then she was pulled against him once more, and she saw over his shoulder that he must have turned back the duvet covering the bed when he had emerged from the bathroom.

'Undress me, Carla,' he was urging harshly against the warm slender column of her neck. 'Untie my robe. I want to feel our bodies together again ... God, I've wanted it so badly!'

But she was mutely defiant, desperately trying to ignore the fiery tide of passion coursing through her, so he did it himself, groaning as skin touched skin, his hardness fitting perfectly against her softness.

Somehow they were together on the bed, and Carla could protest no longer. Revel's hands swept over her body in long, seducing caresses; her breathing became rapid and shallow and she stirred restlessly. Her breasts felt heavy, aching with desire, and there was a molten heat in her loins that made her hips lift, writhing, seeking a greater intimacy. When his mouth touched her breasts she gasped, burying her fingers in his dark hair, the pagan tempo of her pulses driving her to a frenzy of longing. His marauding mouth lingered at her breasts and then moved on, and she touched and kissed him in response, tasting the salt of his perspiration, whimpering with an intolerable desire as she sought the core of his masculinity and heard him gasp in his turn.

His mouth and hands found all the erogenous zones she had never known she had, and she moaned softly as he pressed her back into the mattress and lowered himself on to her, his hot, hard weight a further aphrodisiac. His body hair was harsh against her turgid breasts, making them unbearably sensitive, and his smooth muscled back felt damp and slippery beneath her palms as she stroked and clutched at him with urgent convulsiveness.

'Tell me what you're feeling, Carla,' Revel demanded hoarsely, looking down into her face with glazed eyes, his mouth inches from the vivid pulsating invitation of her swollen lips.

'Hatred,' she spat, appalled.

'But what is your body feeling?' His powerful thighs moved against hers and her desire became an exquisitely searing heat concentrated in one intimate place.

'Pleasure, damn you,' she groaned.

They were both shuddering with desire, clinging together, lost in a welter of erotic sensation, but still Revel didn't take her. His hands began another journey of seduction, straying down from her hips to her thighs, and up again to the satiny secret region of her femininity.

'Revel . . . oh, God, Revel!'

His name was a feverish mutter on her lips, low and continuous, as her traitor body ignored the protests of her humiliated mind. All pride, and self-restraint, were gone; she was totally out of control—more so than Revel because still he didn't take her.

'Tell me what you want,' he commanded tensely, shaking against her. 'Tell me, Carla.'

'You!'

'Then say it.'

'I want you, Revel . . . I want you so much, I can't bear it.'

His dark hard face had a tortured, driven look and was streaming with perspiration, and his hair fell damply over his brow. Carla heard the anguished, sobbing breaths he was drawing. 'I told you you'd beg, didn't I?'

Carla was crying, tears streaming from her eyes as she felt the thrust of his maleness against her. She saw hell in his eyes then, and for the first time she heard him reassuring. 'It will be all right for you this time, Carla, I promise you.'

She arched and gasped, and the ultimate caress was begun, deepening, making them one, and the only things in the world were the damp heat of their clinging loins and the sound of their sharp cries of pleasure and their ragged, tortured breathing. She soared free of the bonds of her own mortality to die and be reborn in the white-heat of a dazzling, searing ecstasy.

Afterwards, though, she turned on to her side with her back to Revel, weeping with bitter shame. She had touched the sun, but she had sold her pride to do so.

She felt Revel move and then the softness of the duvet was covering her. There was a click and the room was plunged into darkness. She flinched as his hand descended on her shoulder.

'Don't, Carla,' he urged in a low voice. 'Please. don't!'

'I can't help it,' she mumbled resentfully and heard him sigh.

'You make me cruel.'

'Will I always be to blame for everything?' she questioned with sad resignation. 'You're naturally cruel, Revel, you don't need me to make you that way . . . I still hate you, you know.'

'I know.'

His hand was removed from her shoulder and Carla felt a pang of regret because its warm weight had been vaguely comforting.

She was too drained to think and fell asleep quickly, waking in the hour before dawn to find herself wrapped

in Revel's arms, the hard warmth of his body at her
back familiar already and somehow protective. Still
dazed with sleep, she turned instinctively, putting up a
hand to touch his face.

'Oh, dear God, Carla,' he breathed regretfully. 'I
can't leave you alone. I know you hate me but I must
have you. Whatever harm I've done to you, isn't this
ample revenge, the knowledge that I'm utterly enslaved
by you? It has never happened to me like this before
and, believe me, I don't enjoy it; I don't enjoy telling
you this. . . .'

His hand was stroking along her inner thigh and
Carla closed her eyes in despair as she was assailed by
the languorous weakness that heralded desire. His
enslavement would have been no revenge had she
wanted such a thing, because her own bondage was far
greater than his, of the heart as well as of the flesh.

Her body betrayed her self-respect over and over
again in the five days that followed. Revel's obsession
continued undiminished and he made love to her with
fiercely compulsive intensity, as if impelled in a driving,
desperate quest for some point he never seemed to
attain. She often sensed in him a despair that matched
her own. It was such a destructive situation, Carla often
thought. They were both being torn apart and she
wondered how long it could last.

Their nights were filled with their gall-bitter passion
and there were a couple of days too, when he swung her
into his arms and carried her to the bedroom. She
learnt to know his strong body better than she did her
own, learnt how to make him gasp, groaning with
pleasure, and to make him call out in the agony of his
urgent desire, and learnt to inflict her own small
punishments for what he was doing to her.

And yet she knew so little of his mind. They were
locked in a prison of mutual hostility, resenting their
dependence on each other, and it made conversation

uneasy. They could go hours without talking to each other, and there were seldom relaxed silences. Even if they did talk, mostly about world affairs since Revel was an obsessive tuner-in to news bulletins, there was still an element of constraint.

The weather was as stormy as their passion during those five days, a wild wind ranging at night and dashing the ocean's waves against the beach and rocks, dying only a little during the days. They both took long walks along the beach, but always separately, and Carla knew that Revel sometimes swam, defying the ferocious currents, though the water was icy at this time of year, making the bones ache and cutting into one like a knife. There was an inherent recklessness in his character which had chosen his career and prompted those mad motorbike rides for which he was notorious, and, watching him turn his face defiantly against the wind when he set out for a walk, Carla realised that her husband needed challenge in his life as simply and basically as he did air to breathe.

Yet he could display an oddly sensitive perceptiveness on occasion. Once when he had taken her into his arms one afternoon, and his kisses and caresses were being accepted without resistance because Carla didn't feel strong enough to contend with the humiliation of ultimately being made to plead, he suddenly held her away from him and scanned her face intently.

'You're not feeling well, are you?'

'I'm sorry. That coffee at lunch.' A combination of tiredness and that indolence which often accompanies pregnancy had made her risk sharing his coffee, too lazy to go to the trouble of making tea as well.

He told her to go and lie down and when she woke up in the late afternoon, he brought her a mug of tea, weak and milkless as she liked it. Somewhat bitterly, she wondered why he was bothering to show such consideration—he couldn't care about their child, he didn't want it, and probably resented it for forcing him into this trap, as he surely regarded their marriage.

'Are you feeling better?' He stood beside the bed, surveying her broodingly as she sipped the tea.

'Yes, thank you,' Carla answered curtly, knowing he was probably only asking because he was wondering how long he would have to refrain from subjecting her to his sexual dominance once more.

'You're so well most of the time, that I tend to forget.' He shrugged idly and she reflected that he probably wished he could forget permanently.

'Oh, yes, unfortunately I'm very healthy,' she mocked satirically. 'So there's not much chance of my having a miscarriage and freeing us both from this . . . this——'

'This hell in which we've trapped each other,' Revel supplied bitterly, and turned and walked out of the room.

A sigh shook Carla. She wished she had gone on resisting him when he had raised the question of marriage, and she wished they were back in Cape Town. The situation might be a little easier there, where they both had their careers to occupy them.

It seemed that Revel was of a similar opinion, reflecting when they awoke on their last morning at the cottage: 'Perhaps we'll . . . hate less, when there are others around us.' He paused, and his voice had hardened when he resumed, 'Tell me, Carla, whom do you hate most, me or yourself?'

She shook her head mutely, dumb with emotion and desire. He was stroking and massaging her tumescent breasts until they were sensitised beyond endurance and her breath came in rapid, heated little gasps.

'No, I don't know either,' Revel agreed harshly, lowering his head to her breasts. And it ended, as she had known it must, with her abject surrender, subjugated beyond bearing and frantically entreating him to possess her.

After all, Carla decided that night, being in Cape Town was going to be no easier, because here she would be haunted by obsessive suspicion and jealousy. Here, Vivienne Franck was within Revel's reach.

Having refused her request for separate bedrooms, he had then left her alone that first night in his beautiful old Rondebosch home, announcing that he was going out. He didn't elaborate on that, and Carla was too reserved to ask, merely inclining her head with a show of indifference.

He had not returned by eleven when she settled Pasht, somewhat nervy at being in a strange house, in what she supposed could be called a morning room since there was another bigger and more formal lounge across the hallway. She dragged out her face cleansing routine and bath, but Revel was still absent when she checked on Pasht once more before going to bed.

Had he gone to Vivienne? The question tormented her as she lay wakeful in the dark and the slow minutes ticked by, each hour a lifetime. She wondered where they met, and how often, and all her relief at the possibility of being exempted from the humiliation of Revel's lovemaking for at least one night evaporated. Carla lay tense and still, picturing him with the blonde woman in his arms, imagining them together.

Jealousy seared her, in its way as shaming as her helpless response to Revel's kisses and caresses. Why did she have to love him so much? He didn't deserve her love and, logically, his treatment of her should have killed it. But love knew no logic and could survive the most savage of blows; it was stronger even than pride.

Oh, God, how many nights would there be like this one? She didn't think she could bear many. Ultimately her heart must betray her as surely as her body had already done and she would sink to the final humiliation of begging Revel for his love, imploring him not to see Vivienne. Then he would have the power to destroy her utterly.

Carla was still awake when Revel finally returned at two o'clock. He didn't switch on any lights as he passed through the big bedroom to the luxurious adjoining bathroom and she remained silent, pretending to be asleep. He would have no compunction about waking her if he wanted her.

But when Revel came to bed, still in the dark, he kept to his own side of the bed, making no move to touch her, and Carla knew by his breathing that he fell asleep very quickly. Then her bitter knowledge was complete, and the silent, scalding tears slipped down her cheeks. Sated after the hours he had spent with Vivienne, he didn't need her. Vivienne was for loving, she merely for dominating.

Early in the morning she was awoken by the telephone at Revel's side of the bed. He listened, said a few curt words, and got out of bed as soon as he had replaced the receiver, not looking at Carla.

When he emerged from the bathroom, he was dressed in jeans and a matching blue shirt, and she knew that their first parting had come. He stood beside the bed, looking at her with moody eyes, his face dark and drawn in the pale early morning light.

'What is it?' she asked.

'Rioting in Soweto. I don't know when I'll be back, possibly after a few days. If the mood up there spreads to places like Langa down here, I want you to avoid going out that way. You know how vulnerable to stoning and overturning people in cars are.' He dropped something on to the low shelf beside her and went on in the same abrupt voice, 'Your set of keys for the house. Ramira Malgas also has a set; she comes in for four-and-a-half days a week, and her husband twice a week to take care of the outdoor maintenance. If there are any of their duties, cooking, cleaning or gardening, that you've a taste for, then discuss it with them, but I certainly don't expect it of you while you're still working, so don't feel you have to take an interest in running things.'

'Thank you,' Carla said huskily, her eyes hungry as they rested on his face, but part of Revel's mind had already flown ahead to the rioting he must cover for *The Courant*, and he was unreceptive to her mood, impatient to say all that needed saying.

'Then, Noelle Malherbe will be coming to see you this morning. You've heard of her? She has been decorating this house for me. I saw her last night and she thinks she could convert a room into a developing room for you without ruining the look of the interior, but naturally the two of you will want to discuss it first. She'd also like to accompany you to your old flat and help you decide which items of your furniture will fit in with what she has already chosen, but don't feel you have to be guided by her. As for a studio—you don't do much studio work, do you? But if you want one, rent one in the city. I think that's all, Carla. I'll see you soon, probably next week.'

He picked up his jacket and an overnight bag he evidently kept ready for such occasions, and then he was striding out of the room—leaving her. Carla wanted to call after him, begging him to take care, but her throat felt constricted with incipient tears. Hurt and resentment tore at her. He hadn't even kissed her, as he would an ordinary wife, a wife he had chosen willingly, and he had committed her to a meeting with Noelle Malherbe without consulting her first. Perhaps he didn't trust her taste. . . .

And it was the interior decorator he had been with last night. Or had he seen Vivienne as well? He had been absent for so long, he could have rendezvoused with several different women, giving them each an hour, but she remained convinced that it was Vivienne who had satisfied him physically and made him so remote with her.

Noelle Malherbe was thirty-two, but she looked ten years younger, a tiny, exquisite woman with huge blue eyes set in a heart-shaped face and long black hair hanging down her slim back. She looked and moved like a dancer, with that classical symmetry of beauty and deceptive air of steel-shot fragility that were the hallmark of all the great prima ballerinas.

Once again, Carla knew scorching jealousy, visualising her in Revel's arms, that long black hair spread across his pillow . . . Noelle had decorated the master bedroom upstairs; had she also slept there?

Reluctantly, Carla had to admit that her taste was superb. Revel's house was one of the old, now much-coveted and valuable double-storey ones in Rondebosch, and Noelle and her team had made it habitable without detracting from its atmosphere of history and grace. The themes of the various rooms flowed harmoniously into each other and, while some items of furniture were the cherished antiques of the old Boland and Western Province, it was still a home in which to relax, complemented by the manicured English-style garden Basheer Malgas had created.

Somewhat to Carla's relief, Noelle was one of those talkative people who failed to be frozen by her own reticence, so no uncomfortable silences fell during the several meetings they had in the next few days. Entirely self-absorbed, Noelle would chatter continuously, skipping from subject to subject, oblivious to all Carla's reactions, whether of pain or amusement.

'Now this chair you say your cat is so attached to. . . . It needs recovering, but we'll do it in the same colour again, I think, and it will look super in the little lounging room which is a good place for a cat as it's sunny. Lucky the animal fits into the colour scheme. Some mongrel cats and dogs just ruin the look of a room, as do grubby kids, but what can you do?' Noelle gestured widely. 'People can't exist without their animals and children, and often in that order. . . . Let's see, what else is there? That gorgeous kitchen table of yours. I've made you an excellent offer, but if you're adamant in refusing to sell it, then it's going to look terrific in the kitchen. Fortunately Mrs Malgas appreciates old things; some domestics won't take a job where the kitchen doesn't shriek with garish plastic, but she's not like that.'

'She's lovely,' Carla agreed quietly, for she felt that the middle-aged Ramira Malgas was a friend already.

'You're lucky to have her. You want someone you can rely on, when your work doesn't leave you much time for domesticity. I must say, I was surprised to hear Rev had got married.' For once, Noelle looked at Carla and actually saw her, though her blue eyes were blank with incomprehension, as if she couldn't understand what Revel had seen in her. 'I suppose it makes sense, in a way. You're both in the same business. If I'd ever thought about it in the past, I would have guessed he'd marry a woman with a demanding career of her own, because he gives so much of himself to his career that there isn't much left for personal relationships. Yes, I would have guessed at someone like you, or myself, but in my case he made it clear right from the start that he would make no long-term commitment. Well, it was great while it lasted. . . . Now, Vivienne Franck wouldn't have suited Rev at all—if she had suddenly found herself free to become a permanent part of his life, he'd have ended the affair quite brutally, I'm sure. . . . Well, I guess he has, anyway, now that he has finally found someone he can face spending the rest of his life with. I'm glad. Vivienne Franck is a first class bitch!'

Noelle's light voice rambled on and on as she examined the contents of the flat, but Carla was no longer listening. She was wrong, she thought anguishedly. Revel hadn't ended his affair with Vivienne. Clearly Noelle was not in possession of all the facts. She was assuming that because Revel had married her, he must love her. But it was Vivienne whom he loved, so the affair couldn't have ended.

As Vivienne Franck herself confirmed a few days later.

CHAPTER EIGHT

REVEL had been away a week when Vivienne visited Carla, and it had been a week of sheer misery. Tired of Noelle Malherbe's somewhat insensitive chatter and depressed by the problems Marigold Vibor kept forecasting, Carla had telephoned Bernard Franck, simply for the sake of hearing a kindly voice.

It had been a mistake. Bernard had happened to mention that his wife was away in Johannesburg, ostensibly attending a film festival, and Carla's suspicions had multiplied and become conviction. Johannesburg. Revel would be based in the reef city while he covered these latest Soweto riots.

She tried desperately to resist the tears that were never far from her these days, feeling that she was being weak and that too much emotional weeping would be bad for the baby who depended on her health for its own wellbeing, but it was a fight she frequently lost and her face had grown thin and wan, her eyes permanently shadowed.

It was a wet and windy evening when Vivienne arrived, and Ramira Malgas had left to catch her bus as soon as Carla had returned from her day's assignment, photographing an impressive power station.

'Can I offer you something to drink?' Carla asked politely as they entered the lounge, Vivienne in the lead, which was revealing. 'It's so cold outside. Tea, coffee, or——'

'Oh, something stronger, for heaven's sake,' Vivienne said sharply, sinking gracefully on to the couch. She gave Carla a distasteful look. 'Scotch. Neat. I suppose our little mother-to-be is religiously abstaining!'

Carla could feel the colour draining from her face, but moments later the hot colour of embarrassment was flooding her cheeks. Revel had discussed her with his mistress, he had told her why they had got married——

'I'm told I can have wine and sherry in moderation,' she offered stiltedly, endeavouring to conceal the resentment that was burning steadily higher within her.

She gave Vivienne the drink she had demanded, fetched a flask of sweet sherry for herself and sat down opposite the woman. The lounge, a truly beautiful room in cream and white with the subtle bronze, peach and palest eau-de-Nil green of the luxurious carpet repeated in such items as cushion covers, was delightfully warm, and Carla felt tired and drowsy as she usually did at this hour since becoming pregnant.

Jealousy added its weight to her habitual shyness and she sat in awkward silence, waiting for Vivienne to speak, but the older woman seemed in no hurry. She glanced disparagingly at Carla, assessing her minimal make-up and the straight olive-green jeans she wore with one of her baggy chenille sweaters, this one olive, gold and cream, and then complacently down at her own two-piece just a few shades lighter than her remarkable eyes and worn with a chic scarlet scarf, and Carla winced at the obvious comparison she was making.

Next those hard inky eyes appraised the room and a slight supercilious smile curved the pouting mouth. 'Ye-es, Noelle Malherbe hasn't done too badly,' she commented patronisingly. 'But I wonder how you like living in a house decorated by one of Revel's ex-lovers, Carla?'

'She's the best in Cape Town,' Carla replied quietly. 'And the décor reflects Revel's taste or he wouldn't have accepted it. It reflects mine as well.'

'You surprise me,' Vivienne drawled. 'She shook her head. 'I can't understand this penchant for old houses. Give me a modern one any day. These old places are supposed to be haunted, did you know? Doesn't it bother you, the thought of Malay-magic and that sort of thing? That Malgas woman has some Malay blood.'

Grateful for this less personal aspect, Carla made a real effort to respond courteously. 'Hasn't it been proved that it's unfair to blame the Malays for all the supernatural events in this part of the world? Most cultures, including our own, have their adherents to some form of witchcraft or another.'

Vivienne shrugged dismissively. 'All the same, I wouldn't fancy being alone here at night—and you'll often be alone, won't you?'

'Revel's job——'

'I wasn't referring to his job.' A vicious note had entered Vivienne's voice. 'How long do you think you can hold Revel's interest—if you haven't already lost it? Sure, you've got this physical chemistry going for you, but that sort of thing palls pretty damn quickly. A man like Revel needs more than that, and a girl like you . . . hell, what can you give him? I can guarantee that when he's at home you'll find that he starts making excuses to go out every night—and guess where he'll be, Carla?'

'Please, I can't . . . I'm sorry, I can't talk about my marriage,' Carla said with a desperate sort of dignity, lifting her head and meeting the older woman's hard blue eyes.

'But that's what I came here to discuss.' Vivienne's smile was malicious. 'I've been with Revel in Johannesburg and he told me everything . . . how neatly you trapped him. Hell, it's the oldest trick in the book, getting pregnant. I suppose you really are pregnant and not just pretending?'

Carla crossed her arms over her body in that defensive gesture that was becoming habitual. 'Revel didn't have to marry me,' she said stiffly and saw Vivienne's lovely face contort and turn momentarily ugly with hatred, but she was too inhibited to continue.

Brought up in an environment where it was deemed bad manners to reveal hostility, she was appalled by Vivienne's naked antipathy.

'I warned you not to let him use you,' Vivienne was continuing venomously. 'But you went ahead, and now he's paying for it—a high price for whatever pleasure he had from you.'

Carla flushed. 'Please, go ... just go away,' she requested in a low, strained voice, hands tense while her bright lips were quivering and her eyes piteous.

There was a short silence as Vivienne eyed her scornfully. Then, 'You poor fool, you're in love with him.'

Carla couldn't reply. She was fighting a rising feeling of nausea and had no energy for anything else.

'And I've got him. I've got the man you want!' Vivienne's voice rang with triumph as she stood up. 'How does it feel to know that, Carla? He's mine, and he always will be.'

A slight sound at the door leading to the hall made them both look in that direction. Carla felt dizzy, unable to stand up lest she faint. In dark clothes, Revel stood there, smiling with some irony.

Vivienne seemed as disconcerted as she, but her recovery was swifter. 'Revel! Have you just got back? Ships that pass ... I was on the point of leaving, but I'll be seeing you?'

'Of course. I'll see you out,' Revel offered urbanely with the briefest of glances for the motionless Carla.

She stood up carefully when they had gone outside, and walked into the hall, moving slowly, like an old woman, she thought anguishedly. How much had Revel heard and would he realise she loved him? Ah, God, she couldn't bear it!

The front door opened, admitting a gust of chill evening air, and Revel came in, slamming it shut. He stood still, looking at Carla, and she began to shake, taking an involuntary step backwards which he noted with a tightening of his mouth. Tall and darkly menacing, he had a wild, reckless look, and the aura of aggressiveness emanating from him threatened her.

Slanting blue-green eyes hardened as they noted her pale, distressed face and the emotional brightness of her eyes. His lips twisted sardonically.

'What has upset you, Vivienne's visit or my return? Take comfort, Carla, she may have what you want, but equally you've got what she wants—and how!' His voice sank bitterly. 'My God, and how you have!'

The chill in Carla's heart intensified. As Vivienne had said and as she herself had anticipated, his resentment of being trapped in a loveless, unwanted marriage was growing.

'I'm sorry,' she murmured numbly.

His sharp glance slashed her face. 'Why don't you have an early night? I'm going out and I don't know when I'll be back.'

'Where . . . where are you going?' She sounded like the archetypal clinging wife, Carla realised with acidic self-contempt.

'To Chapman's Peak. I'm taking the Honda.'

Her blood ran icy at the thought. A high wind would be blowing on the coastal road and the drizzle that had been falling for most of the day would have made the surface of that winding road slick and dangerous.

'If . . . if you stayed, I could make you some supper . . . dinner,' she ventured tentatively, desperate to keep him with her.

'Forget it.' The light in his eyes was savage. 'If I stayed, we'd both regret it . . . as we did once before.'

The night he had first made love to her, Carla recalled bleakly, watching him swing away from her, noting the quick tension of his movements that spoke of a barely suppressed violence.

She waited until he had gone before stumbling into

the downstairs cloakroom and being sick. Afterwards she sat trembling on the second step of the staircase that rose from the hall, waiting for strength to return to her shivering limbs.

She ought to make herself something to eat, for the baby's sake at least, but she couldn't move. She knew she would not be able to relax until Revel had returned safely from his wild ride. She thought she could have accepted the dangers he faced in the course of his work without protesting, knowing that a man's work was part of himself, but this extra, needless risk he took destroyed her.

She would rather endure humiliation in his arms than have him risk his life outdistancing his daemons on that terrifying machine of his, and yet she hadn't been able to tell him so. How could she? He would guess that she cared, loved, and then his power over her would be absolute and perhaps his hatred even stronger because deep within himself he would feel guilty, and consequently, resentful.

Eventually she made her way to the kitchen where she made tea for herself and ate a couple of little la vache qui rit cheeses, but fear and despair haunted her all that evening. When, after several hours, Revel had not returned, she had to fight against the impulse to telephone hospitals and the traffic department, knowing that if he was all right, he would be furious to learn what she had done.

He had probably gone on to meet Vivienne somewhere, she surmised achingly. They could have arranged it when he had seen her out earlier. She wondered where they made love. The Franck home was a possibility since Bernard often stayed at the Franck Constructions offices until late at night, even past midnight sometimes. She felt sorry for him, and even sorrier for herself and her child, unwanted by its father, resented. . . .

Much later, when she was huddled in bed, torturing herself with visions of Revel's beautiful, beloved body lying smashed and broken and bleeding, or flung over a cliff edge into the icy ocean, she heard the sound of the Honda, shattering the quiet of the night. Her immediate relief gave way almost instantly to a bitter resentment. He was selfish and callous and inconsiderate, but how could she tell him so without giving herself away?

Thus, she was once more pretending to be asleep when he came to bed, and yet she was almost disappointed when he didn't reach for her, feeling that for once she could have successfully resisted him, her anger providing her with the necessary strength of mind.

In the morning, she faced him with a stiffly unresponsive face, her replies stilted if he addressed her, and Revel's own eyes were cool for once.

'You look a wreck,' he stated brutally when he emerged from the bathroom to find her propped up against the pillows, listening to the news on the radio beside the bed. 'You aren't sleeping. . . . You were pretending when I got back, and the same that last night I spent here. Have you told your doctor?'

'I slept perfectly well while you were away,' Carla lied and blushed a little. Something was shifting within her, altering focus, and she knew an uncharacteristic desire to wound him in retaliation for all the hurt he had dealt her.

'So what keeps you awake when I'm here?' Revel taunted.

'Well, not expectation anyway,' Carla informed him scathingly. 'Fear might be nearer the mark.'

His freshly shaven face darkened. 'But as it turned out, you had nothing to fear.'

'No,' she agreed. Not while he was seeing Vivienne. She added mockingly, 'I'm grateful.'

Revel laughed harshly, but his eyes remained cool,

and Carla looked away, feeling a tightening in her breast as if an iron band were closing inexorably about her heart. What had happened to the torrid, obsessive desire he had felt for her little more than a week ago? Had it burned itself out so quickly? Certainly, it had been a destructive, consuming thing, and as Vivienne had pointed out yesterday, mere lust was not a durable thing. Or was he being faithful to his beloved Vivienne? She could have demanded that of him, or he might simply have reassessed his values and decided that his love for his mistress was of infinitely greater worth than his physical reaction to his unwanted wife.

Keeping her eyes downcast, Carla ventured shyly, 'When . . . when will you have to go away again?'

'You'll have to put up with me for, perhaps, a week, if that's what you're asking,' Revel responded silkily.

'It's not . . . I didn't mean . . . oh, God!' Carla concluded despairingly and he laughed softly.

'I know exactly what you meant.'

He strode out of the room and Carla got wearily out of bed. If she was this tired now, what would she be like by tonight? Perhaps she ought to talk to Dr Basson, but what could he recommend? She doubted if sleeping tablets were prescribed for pregnant women, and even if they were, she didn't want to take the risk.

She showered, and dressed in cream jeans, russet legwarmers and a soft matching velour top in a long style that hid the waistband she had left unbuttoned. She ought to think about buying some maternity clothes, she supposed. Perhaps she would go shopping after her lecture this afternoon.

Going downstairs, she found Revel at the kitchen table, drinking coffee as he perused the morning newspaper, while Pasht ate her cat biscuits from a dish on the floor.

'Don't you want breakfast?' she asked, switching on the kettle to make tea for herself.

'Not unless you'll cook it for me,' he answered drily. 'I don't enjoy preparing food for myself.'

'I'll do Dutch pancakes. You liked them when I made them at your cottage, didn't you? What did you do before you had a wife?' she added tartly, then flushed, realising that he had probably always woken up with a woman who would undoubtedly have been only too willing to provide him with breakfast.

Revel noted the colour in her cheeks and looked amused, but he merely said mildly, 'Ramira always stocked the freezer with things like waffles which take only a few minutes to heat.'

'Bad for you,' she said lightly, extracting bacon from the fridge.

'So are Dutch pancakes.'

'You won't be getting them every day, that's for sure!'

He watched her for a while before questioning idly, 'You enjoy cooking, don't you?'

'Yes. My mother taught me. Like all Karoo farmer's wives, she's an amazing cook. So is my sister-in-law.'

'Have you told your family about the baby yet?'

'Not yet. I'm too much of a coward to face my parents' pain, their distress ... But you wouldn't understand that, would you, Revel? You'll never shrink from hurting anyone, you'll never consider the sensitivity of people whose mores are different, who are more easily shocked. . . . But I'd rather be a coward!'

'You really hate me, don't you?'

'Yes!' And it was partly true.

'Too bad, Carla,' he drawled in a hard voice. 'We're married, and there's this baby ... I regret the whole affair as much as you do, but there's no escape for either of us. Our child deserves at least the comfort of knowing that we tried to give it a conventional start in life.'

'Neither of us seems to be trying very hard,' Carla offered in a small, quivering voice.

'No.' Revel's voice was flat now, and she turned to look at him in some surprise. He grimaced. 'It's all so much more bloody difficult than I anticipated. Where do we even begin?'

'We can't even hold a normal, civilised conversation,' Carla agreed, guiltily wondering how much her reserve was to blame for that. She was only eloquent when angry or resentful.

'Try.... For instance, have you been busy in the last week?'

'Just lecturing, and a couple of assignments. I've spent a lot of time with Noelle Malherbe.... You'll have noticed the additional furnishings?'

'Yes. Who else have you seen?'

'The people at *Afrinews*, that's all. And Vivienne last night.'

'Not Bernard Franck?' Revel was watching her and Carla's face closed.

'No. I did telephone him, though,' she added with a touch of defiance.

'Why?'

'Is that your business? If you must know, I wanted to speak to someone . . . kind,' she brought out pointedly, abandoning any attempt to sound pleasant because Revel's stare was unnerving her.

'I get the implication,' he responded tautly. 'I don't want you seeing him, Carla.'

She looked at him scornfully. His attitude toward Bernard was incomprehensible, but she supposed it had something to do with Vivienne. He was forced to share Vivienne with Bernard, and he didn't want to share his wife as well—however innocently, however little personal regard he had for her. Resentful contempt for all men welled up inside her. They were so possessive, so hypocritical—it was all right for Revel to continue his affair with Vivienne, but she wasn't permitted even an innocent friendship with Bernard.

'If you want a civilised conversation, leave Bernard out of it, since you can't be rational about him,' she advised. 'Will you want maple syrup with your pancakes?'

'No, thanks.' His face was inscrutable now. 'Are you working today?'

'A lecture this afternoon.'

'Do you want to go down to the cottage for the weekend?'

Carla stiffened. 'No,' she said baldly, all finesse deserting her. She couldn't face that again. Without Vivienne's nearby presence to deter him, he would subject her to his lovemaking again, and she knew that if he did, she would end up begging not only for his possession, but for his love as well.

'Why not?'

'Because . . . because I hated . . . Oh, God!' Why were words so difficult, so dangerous? She flushed at the anger flaring in Revel's eyes.

'Don't say any more unless you want me to take you upstairs and prove to you that you never did and never will hate my lovemaking, Carla,' he advised savagely, pouring himself another cup of coffee.

'No, I'll tell you what it was that I hated,' she volunteered heatedly. 'It was the fact that you always deliberately set out to humiliate me. Or have you conveniently put that out of your mind, Revel? You made me . . . beg, remember?'

'You made me cruel,' he retorted. 'With your hypocritical reluctance. I wanted you and you wanted me, and——'

'Wanting!' Carla cut in bitterly. 'That's where you and I are furthest apart. You see it as completely natural to find physical gratification without love, but to me wanting without loving is sick and . . . and sordid and degrading, and that's why I . . . I try to resist it, even if you make damned sure that I never succeed. I hate and despise myself for being so weak as to let you seduce me and dominate me like that ... I wish to God I'd never married you.'

'Why did you?'

'I don't know. You were harassing me, I was tired, I didn't know what else to do ... I suppose I was thinking of my parents,' she concluded wearily.

She had also been thinking of their child, but she didn't want to tell him that and see the bitter resentment harden his face. And she supposed her love for him had had something to do with it as well. She could remember thinking she might make something of their marriage, beginning by making him sexually dependent on her, but that was before she had realised that sex untouched by love could never be enough for her.

Revel was regarding her with a bitterness she knew would be reflected in her own eyes.

'It's no use, is it?' he offered tonelessly. 'Everything brings us back to our forced marriage and the reason for it. We're nicely trapped, aren't we?'

She turned away in silence, overwhelmed by a sense of utter futility. He was right, they were trapped together, floundering in a turbid morass of acrimony, and as each of them sank deeper, they would fight to drag the other down as well.

There was no escape.

A miasma of misery enveloped Carla in the days that followed, choking her with its acrid poison. There was just no common meeting point between Revel and herself, and the silence between them thickened with tension.

Despairing unhappiness stalked her, denying her any pleasure. Even when she flew to the Transvaal for half a day to take photos at a massive steel works, normally one of her favourite subjects, she found her usual excitement diminished.

Revel too was working by day although he was at home. Recent riots and bomb blasts had made the South African political scene topical again, and he was preparing some high-powered reports and interviews for overseas broadcasting corporations for which he was an occasional stringer, somewhat unorthodoxly, as Nathaniel Nash often pointed out, Revel told her, but once again *The Courant*'s proprietor was not prepared to risk losing him by complaining too vehemently.

Carla felt permanently tense those days, torn between yearning and fear. She longed to know again the urgent power of Revel's body in hers, and yet she dreaded the humiliation of her unmistakable response to a man who didn't love her. Most of all, though, she ached, pitifully for just some small sign of concern from her husband, just the slightest show of caring. Sometimes she felt so coldly alone, bereft of all that was warm and gentle and kind, and her need for tenderness became a perpetual agony.

But she could arouse nothing of that nature in Revel just as, these days, she couldn't arouse his passion either, and she knew why. Vivienne Franck was satisfying him. As the other woman had predicted, he had some excuse for going out every night. Usually Carla didn't even listen to it, knowing it would be a lie, and at least she still possessed sufficient pride to prevent her imploring him to stay with her.

Even tonight he had gone out, she reflected resentfully on her sixth night alone since his return from covering the Soweto riots. He had come home earlier, though, bringing a visiting Reuters man who had been a colleague in the days when they had both been gaining Fleet Street experience. The two of them had drunk quite a lot and talked long, so that it was late when the visitor had departed, but still Revel had gone out—

without even proffering an excuse this time, Carla remembered angrily.

He didn't want her, and yet this morning, when she had ventured to ask again if they couldn't have separate bedrooms, his reply had been inexorable: 'No. You're my wife, Carla, you share my bed.'

Only she wasn't sharing it. She was alone—and there was that noise again. It was muffled and unidentifiable, but she was convinced that it came from somewhere inside the house. The only trouble was, she was insufficiently well acquainted with the house to be able to pinpoint it. In fact, her hearing might be deluding her, because it had seemed to come from a different direction this time.

Wide-eyed, Carla lay absolutely still, staring into the darkness, as if by keeping her eyes open, her ears might function better. She was too afraid to switch the light on, lest the sounds had a human origin and the light attracted the intruder.

That muffled thud sounded again, this time accompanied by a faint tinkle, like wind chimes, remote and ethereal, as if the sound came from another dimension. She had giggled over the weird special effects in half a dozen supposedly chilling films, but now they suddenly seemed quite possible in real life, quite realistic. . . .

Cautiously, Carla sat up, realising that she was sweating with terror. The mattress was too good a one to creak, but every slight sound she made seemed amplified, the brush of her silk nightdress against her legs, her own breathing. . . .

Realising it, she held her breath as she got slowly out of bed and made her way on bare feet to the bedroom door, pausing after each frightened step to strain her ears for sounds, beginning to imagine them now.

The key was in the door and very, very slowly, she turned it, her pulses leaping madly when it clicked slightly. Though what use was a locked door, if the house was haunted?

She wanted to giggle hysterically, sitting on the edge of the bed, wondering what to do next. Lock herself in the bathroom as an extra precaution? No. . . .

Anger was beginning to mingle with her fear, gnawing at her until her cheeks grew hot. Revel had no right to go out night after night unless he was covering a story, leaving her alone here in a house that still felt strange. She was acting a wifely role, cooking for him when he was here, yielding to his demand that she share this bed, so he owed her something in return. He couldn't have it all his own way and, damn it, she was pregnant and surely merited a little concern.

The thought of the life cradled within her body calmed her a little. So much unhappiness and now this sheer, stark terror couldn't be good for the baby.

But it was Revel's child as well; he had a responsibility towards it, she reminded herself furiously. She was angry with herself for being so afraid and helpless, but she was succeeding in turning that anger against Revel. Vivienne Franck could damn well do without him for once; his place was here with her, protecting her and investigating that noise, and she would demand that he return at once. For once in her life, Carla was going to stand on a right.

The trouble was, she had no idea where to contact him, but just in case she was misjudging him, she would try *The Courant* first. Still in the dark, she reached for the telephone at Revel's side of the bed and carefully lifted the receiver, rehearsing the number she already knew, having had some dealings with *The Courant* in the past. She dialled by touch alone and got an instant reply from someone on the night staff, but they could tell her nothing of Revel's whereabouts when she asked in a low voice if he was out on a story.

'I can give you his home number if it's urgent, or would you like to speak to someone else on our staff?'

'No ... no, thank you.' Carla replaced the receiver. Her low voice had probably sounded conspiratorial and they must have thought she was someone ringing to tip him off about a pre-dawn raid or some such thing.

So what did she do now? Where did Revel and Vivienne have their illicit meetings? A flat, a hotel, or at the Franck home? It could only be about eleven-thirty now, and Bernard was probably still at his office, courting ulcers, so they might well be at the house. It was the only number she knew to try, anyway.

To her horror, Bernard's voice greeted her, and she gulped, realising that she hadn't considered this contingency, and what could she say without alerting him to Vivienne's infidelity?

'Bernard ... It ... it's Carla. I was just wondering ... Revel? He isn't visiting you, is he? I want him to come home and——'

'No, I'm afraid he's not here, Carla,' Bernard told her, apparently unsuspecting. 'He doesn't visit us that often despite the fact that he and Vivienne grew up together. Was it urgent? Have you tried his paper? Carla ... Carla, are you still there?'

Carla was holding the receiver away from her ear, listening tensely to a different sound this time, but still coming from somewhere inside the house, downstairs she thought. It was a faint banshee wailing, as distantly eerie as that earlier tinkling had been, and it froze her blood.

'Oh, God, there are noises in the house, that's why I wanted Revel ... Bernard, it's not human, not burglars, I mean, and I'm frightened!'

'I'll come over,' he said promptly. 'Just as soon as I've called our housekeeper over to the house so that Justine has someone with her. My wife is out. Meanwhile, lock yourself in somewhere safe, Carla, and keep trying to contact Revel. If you change your mind and think it's an intruder, call the police. Can you be brave enough to let me in when I arrive?'

'I . . . I think so.'

'I'll be with you as soon as I can. Try not to panic. You've probably left a window open and the wind is moving something.'

But the sounds were too varied, too irregular for that. Carla replaced the receiver and dived under the duvet, stopping her ears against those noises. If she couldn't hear them, perhaps they would stop in reality. Her heart was thundering painfully, and the seconds dragged by while she tried to work out how far Bernard would have got on the short drive from Bishopscourt. She knew the route and could visualise every block. . . .

Another thought crept into her mind. Vivienne was out, he had said. And Revel was out. Well, she had guessed they were together, hadn't she, so why the hell was she crying? She was always crying these days, and Revel just wasn't worth it. She was weak and stupid and cowardly. . . .

Panic and misery made her shoulders heave as she tried to stifle her sobs. She huddled under the duvet, frightened, angry and desperately unhappy.

CHAPTER NINE

It seemed an age before Carla heard the quiet sound of Bernard's BMW. She got out of bed, pulled on her velour robe and then hesitated, summoning all her courage before unlocking the bedroom door.

She was probably being stupidly hysterical, but she dared not switch on any lights, and she went barefoot for fear of making a sound. She made slow progress in the dark, not yet sufficiently familiar with the house to be able to find her way by instinct, and she kept pausing, expecting to hear those earlier blood-curdling sounds again, but now the house was absolutely silent. She didn't know what she would do if that banshee wailing started again while she was so exposed—scream or faint, she supposed.

Her heart flipped in terror as she heard the heavy knocker descend against the front door, followed by Bernard's voice, calling her name and reassuring her that it was he. She felt desperately vulnerable, totally unprotected, here on the stairs, and when she reached the hall, her nerve snapped and she flew across it to unlock the door with clumsy, scrabbling fingers.

'Oh, Bernard, I'm so glad you've come . . . I've been so frightened!' she exclaimed wildly as he stepped into the hall, steadying her by placing his hands on her arms.

'There's no need to be now,' he reassured her sympathetically, his eyes widening with slight shock as he registered her pale, tear-streaked face and the feverish glaze of her eyes. 'God, poor Carla, what an experience to have. Never mind, we'll investigate together and we'll probably find some perfectly harmless explanation for whatever you heard. Darkness distorts sounds, you know, and so does fear. . . . Have the noises continued?'

'I . . . I think so. I blocked my ears,' she admitted, beginning to feel embarrassed.

Bernard closed the front door and she wondered if that was wise—they might be needing to escape.

Did you manage to contact Revel? Do . . . My God!' Bernard stopped as an unearthly, disembodied wailing rent the air. 'What the hell is that?'

Carla's fingertips were pressed to her lips and she was trembling after the shock of hearing that sound, but closer to its source, she was beginning to realise what it was.

'Oh, no! Bernard,' she gasped shakily. 'I think . . . I think I've made a terrible fool of myself and brought you here for nothing! But where——'

'What is it?' he repeated, still looking startled. 'It sounds like . . . hell, nothing on earth! Unless you keep peacocks and geese in your house!'

'I think, I know . . . it's Pasht!' Carla laughed, a purely nervous reaction. 'But where can she be? I don't remember . . . Oh, God, Bernard, I think I must be losing my mind! I don't remember shutting her up in the little lounge as I always do. I've never forgotten before!'

'Calm down, Carla,' he advised gently. 'Anyone can forget. Let's find her, shall we? It sounds as if she's shut up somewhere and can't get out. Where did you last see her?'

'In there.' Carla gestured agitatedly towards the big, more formal lounge. 'Revel had a friend here earlier this evening and Pasht took a liking to him. She was weaving around his ankles just before he left. I went into the hall with them and didn't come back in here again. Revel would have put the lights out before he went out.'

'And perhaps inadvertently shut Pasht in somewhere.' Bernard located the light switch and then stood looking round the room. 'Ah, yes!'

Two deep comfortable sofas stood at right angles in the corner containing the beautiful and discreet drinks cabinet Noelle Malherbe had acquired for Revel at an antiques auction, forming an intimate conversation nook. Bernard strode to the cabinet, trying first the side which contained the bottles, then the one where the glasses were kept, and this one yielded the ruffled, highly indignant cat.

'Poor little Pasht,' he laughed, but with compassion, as she leapt out, shaking herself. 'No harm done except to her dignity, and I'm afraid she has broken a crystal glass.'

That faint tinkling sound she had heard! Suddenly it all seemed too much for Carla, and this embarrassment coming on top of her earlier unhappiness and fear put her emotions into overload. She burst into tears.

'Oh, poor Pasht, how could I be so thoughtless?' she choked bitterly as Bernard drew her against him and patted her shoulder awkwardly. 'She has been so unsettled, having to leave the flat, and she keeps hiding in cupboards. . . . And I didn't think, I just didn't think . . . I didn't even feed her tonight. How could I. . . . Oh, what's wrong with me?'

'Hush, Carla, don't cry like this. You're under a strain, by the look of you, that's why it slipped your mind,' Bernard comforted, rocking her gently as if she were a child. 'You're probably just as unsettled as Pasht. You've made a sudden, drastic change in your life, getting married, which always requires a period of adjustment; plus, you're continuing with your job. . . . It's nothing unusual to be forgetful. Once, when Justine was a baby, Vivienne put her out in the garden in her pram during the afternoon and clean forgot about her until she woke and cried as we were having dinner. It can happen to anyone.'

'Sorry,' Carla gasped, making a desperate effort to control herself, afraid of blurting out the entire sum of the misery that was engulfing her, and why should Bernard suffer the hurt of knowing his wife was having an affair with Revel? 'I'm all right now.'

He made her sit down on one of the sofas and poured her a glass of Revel's brandy, suggesting she needed it. Not wanting to refuse it and have to tell him she was pregnant, Carla pretended to sip it, its fragrance making her feel slightly faint, and then put the glass down.

Bernard sat beside her and began joking lightly about Pasht who was on the carpet, giving herself a vigorous washing after her traumatic experience, and then moved on to talk about Justine whom he believed had become more stable and mature in recent weeks. Carla knew he was giving her time to collect her composure, and was deeply grateful, but after a while, she said:

'Bernard, it must be terribly late and I've dragged you over her for nothing, as it turns out. Hadn't you better be getting home? Your housekeeper can't appreciate having to sit up this late.'

'As it happens, my wife would have relieved her almost immediately unless she was planning on going out again. As I was driving out to come over here, Vivienne was driving in, and I stopped and explained matters to her,' Bernard informed her.

Which meant that Revel might arrive at any minute.

Even as she thought it, Carla heard the sound of the front door, and sudden agitation brought her to her feet. Only now did she recall Revel's injunction that she wasn't to see Bernard. He would be angry, and she didn't think she could cope with that. Not tonight. She could only pray that he would delay the inevitable interrogation until after Bernard had left, else how could she explain that she had telephoned the Franck residence in the expectation that he would be there with

Vivienne? To do that would be to inflict on Bernard the knowledge of his wife's infidelity, and she wanted to spare him pain. He was so kind. . . .

'What are you doing here, Franck?' Revel rasped from the doorway.

He looked wholly satanic, in black clothes and with his face dark with a lethal fury as he advanced into the room.

'Braden . . .' Bernard's conventional greeting died on his lips.

'Revel, it's my fault,' Carla said hastily, moving quickly towards him on bare feet, terrified that he was going to hit Bernard. 'I telephoned Bernard and asked him to come over . . . I was frightened, you see, and——'

'Yes?' The single word had all the sharp deadliness of a dagger point. Blue-green eyes glittered with a brilliant fury as they raked her contemptuously, assimilating her pale tear-stained face, her robe and bare feet. 'Now who the hell is that?'

The front door knocker had sounded, startling them all, and Revel turned automatically and went back into the hall. Carla followed, hoping for an opportunity to explain to him without Bernard hearing, but in the hall she froze when she saw who he had just admitted.

'Revel, darling, I believe my husband is here?' In an exquisite high-necked velvet dress with a swirling pattern in grey, green and blue, Vivienne Franck was smiling disarmingly. Her eyes went to the petrified Carla and she laughed. 'I admit it, I was curious, and I also wondered if I could help in any way.'

'This is turning into quite a party,' Revel muttered sardonically. 'Come into the lounge, Vivienne, and we'll all have a drink together and be . . . civilised!'

'Excuse me,' Carla murmured and turned towards the stairs, unable to face watching them together. As it was, she had glimpsed the hot, covetous sensuality in

Vivienne's eyes when she looked at Revel.

Behind her, as she ascended the stairs, she was conscious of Revel ushering Vivienne into the lounge.

She went into the bathroom and stared at herself in the mirror above the vanity unit. She looked a wreck, she thought disgustedly, spent and white, and certainly, she had never felt so drained in her life. The simplest thought processes required an effort beyond her strength at that moment.

She splashed her face with cool water, then went into the bedroom and stood before the dressing-table mirror, brushing her silky brown hair, which was getting quite long now, she noted absently. The house was well heated in winter, but she noticed that her feet were cold, so she found the elegant red mules she had bought to go with her robe and slipped them on.

When she looked up, Revel was standing in the doorway, staring at her with blazing eyes, his face set in a hard mask.

'Have ... have they gone?' she asked nervously, though she knew they hadn't.

'No, they're downstairs having a drink and waiting for their hostess to join them,' he retorted harshly.

'Revel. . . .'

'Come, my dear, faithful wife, we have guests to entertain.'

'Revel, I can't——'

'Who are you afraid of facing, Carla? Vivienne or myself?' Revel taunted, grasping her by the wrist and pushing her towards the door.

In the passage she was able to free herself because he was suddenly no longer concentrating on her. He was frozen, looking back into the bedroom, noting the state of the bed which bore witness to her earlier occupancy. Then he looked at her, and the rage in his eyes was so violent that Carla quailed, taking a few quick steps away from him.

'My God! In my bed, and when you're carrying my child! You slut!' Revel's voice was little more than a whisper.

'No! Revel, we didn't, I didn't——' Carla began desperately. 'I telephoned Bernard because I was scared, and I was trying to find you——'

'Can't you think of a better lie than that?' he derided. 'Or perhaps that's the excuse you used to get him to come over here? You didn't need one, Carla, he'd have come anyway. And so, you've seduced him at last. I suppose now that you're an experienced married woman, he no longer had any scruples about taking you.'

'Can't we.... All right, I'll go downstairs, Revel. Let's leave it until they've gone to ... to discuss this. Please!'

By then, perhaps, some of his anger would have abated and he would be more rational, more prepared to listen. She walked along to the top of the stairs, then turned, aware of him following.

He came prowling after her, looking as savage and untamed as the wildest jungle animal. Vaguely stirring at the back of her mind was a sense of injustice—he was having an affair with Vivienne and yet he was furious because he thought Bernard had made love to her. Carla's head drooped. What was the use of pleading and protesting? He never listened to her, never believed her....

Revel didn't halt until he was very close to her, within touching distance, and Carla felt faint, overwhelmed by the raw bitterness of his anger which was destroying them both.

'And why have you been crying? Have you been playing on his sympathy with stories of your brutal husband?' Revel taunted hoarsely. 'My God, before I've finished with you, you'll realise you had nothing to complain about before.'

Thinking he was going to strike her, Carla moved hastily to evade him. Her foot caught in the hem of her robe and she felt herself falling—and falling. Her head was filled with the sound of her own scream and Revel's urgent exclamation, and every stair she hit jarred her body until she came to rest, a limp heap in the hall.

Strangely, she was conscious, and even more strangely, she felt no pain. She lay in a dark place, listening to the voices floating about her.

'Christ!' That was Revel, breathing the Name, close to her, and then adding sharply, 'The telephone in the study, Franck . . . an ambulance.'

She heard Bernard rushing away, and now Vivienne was saying smoothly, 'Revel, there's something important I should tell you.'

Carla wanted to protest. He couldn't give his attention to Vivienne, not now, when she needed him so badly. She tried to lift herself and tell him so.

Then there was pain, rending her, and a terrible coldness inside her. It was that coldness that made her cry out, a mother's instinct telling her what it was.

'No-o-o!' The cry of protesting agony rang through the hall and then, mercifully, she dropped into the black void of unconciousness.

She had been lucky, they told her at the hospital. None of her injuries was serious. A crack on the head caused her severe headaches for a few days, she was badly bruised about her body, and she had dislocated her right wrist and thumb, plus a couple of fingers on each hand in her attempts to stop her fall by clutching at the stairs.

She didn't need to be told that there was no longer going to be a baby.

Carla was in a private ward, a light, warm room brightened by the arrangement of flowers that stood under the window. Marigold Vibor had picked and

arranged her own offering, but Mrs Du Plessis, Noelle
Malherbe and the editor and staff of *Afrinews* had sent
conventional florists' arrangements, and even Nathaniel
Nash had sent flowers with a card containing a
moralistic verse. Ramira and Basheer Malgas had sent a
beautiful arrangement of dried fruit, but there was
nothing from her husband or the Francks.

In contrast to the room her body inhabited, there was
a room in her mind that was grey and empty, a blank
space. She lay in the high bed and stared at nothing, her
eyes expressionless. She didn't think or feel—she
couldn't. It was as if some defence mechanism was
numbing her, waiting until she had the strength to cope
with anguish.

When the doctors and nursing staff asked her how
she was feeling, she replied that she was cold, and the
heating was turned up. It made no difference, though,
because the coldness lay within her, where once a tiny
warm life had quickened.

She answered courteously when she was spoken to,
and she tried to smile at the nurses and ward maids
because it was only polite to show gratitude, but she
never smiled at the man who came to see her in the
evenings—because he never smiled at her.

He never spoke either, and he never sat down. He
would just stand there beside the bed for a while,
staring down at her with a bitter, brooding anger. His
dark face seemed carved from granite and his mouth
was harsh, but Carla was no longer frightened of him.
He was her husband and she knew she loved him, but
that particular agony was also suspended for the time
being, obliterated by the enveloping numb chill that was
her first reaction to a loss that would later bring
unbearable grief.

She was relieved that he didn't want to talk, having
an idea that when he did speak, pain would come back.
Already she was aware that her indifference to everyone

and everything had a flaw in it, because there was a faint, fluttering reaction in her breast whenever he arrived, and a vague curiosity stirred in her mind—why was he so angry now, when the reason for their marriage was gone? He was free. . . .

Then, on the third evening, he said abruptly, 'I'm told you refused to talk to the hospital psychologist today?'

'I didn't refuse. I . . . just told her I didn't think. . . . You see, she said it was part of her job to come round to all mothers who have. . . .' Carla stared blankly at the wall opposite her, before forcing the words out: 'Mothers who have lost their babies. She helps them adjust to . . . to it, but she said I was under no compulsion to talk to her, so I. . . .'

It had been too soon. She didn't want to be forced into facing her bereavement. Not yet. Maybe later on, she would be grateful for someone who could help her get things in perspective, but for the time being she wanted to stay numb and emotionless.

'No, you didn't need her services because you don't feel it as a loss, do you? It's exactly what you planned.' The note of suppressed rage in Revel's voice made Carla's eyes fly to his face and she found it more darkly bitter than she had ever seen it before. 'I was wrong when I thought you'd got Franck over to the house to make love to you. . . . What you did was a damned sight worse than mere unfaithfulness. It was murder, Carla— you killed my child. Oh, yes, you told me the truth when you said you'd contacted him because you were frightened. . . . Frightened by the measures you'd taken to bring on a miscarriage.'

'Revel, no!' Appalled by the terrible accusation, Carla felt her numbness receding. It was as if she had cracked wide open and now anguish was flooding through her; she was drowning in it. 'I wouldn't . . . . How can you . . .? Oh, God!'

'And I'd have been none the wiser, except that your faith in Franck's discretion was misplaced,' Revel continued savagely, though his voice was low. 'He met Vivienne as he was leaving to go to you and told her what you had done. She felt obliged to pass it on to me when you threw yourself down those stairs.'

'I fell down the stairs,' Carla insisted desperately. 'I thought you were going to hit me and——'

'When have I ever hit you?' he interrupted flatly.

Carla stared at him hopelessly, seeing the bleak hatred in his blue-green eyes, and realising that pain lay at the back of it.

'I didn't know you wanted the baby,' she said sadly.

'Why the hell do you think I married you? Not want my own child.' Revel's laugh was mirthless, a hollow sound with echoes of hell. 'You must think I'm unnatural.'

The emptiness had returned to Carla's eyes as despair overwhelmed her. What was the use of protesting? He would never believe her and he would always believe Vivienne. What did it matter, anyway? Now that there was no longer going to be a baby, the reason for their marriage had ceased to exist. They would get a divorce—Carla turned her face away. She just wanted him to be gone, before she gave way to the grief that was raging through her like a storm.

'Go away,' she whispered. 'Please!'

There was a brief silence and she could feel his eyes on her. Then he said harshly, 'I'm going. The psychologist has recommended that you be allowed other visitors, but don't expect Franck. I've told him to keep away from you and if he tries to see you, I'll kill him.'

Carla barely registered the threat. He had gone just in time and now she was being dragged relentlessly down into a vortex of sorrow, weeping bereftly, not only for herself but for Revel too, because he had also wanted their baby and she had never even known it. A drenching anguish had her in its possession. Now there was no baby and there would be no second chance because there was no need for their marriage to continue. Everything, hope and joy, were obliterated for all time in the holocaust brought about by circumstances and the diabolically cruel opportunism of Vivienne Franck.

'Nothing!' Carla sobbed aloud.

Nothing was left except her love for Revel, and even that was flawed with its dark side of hatred, while pure hatred was all he felt for her. He would never trust, never believe her. . . .

When a nurse came in a short while later, she found her patient almost hysterical with grief and running a high temperature.

She was sedated for the night and when she woke in the morning, there were no more tears. Her despair was silent, resigned to permanent agony. Outwardly, she was as calm and unforthcoming as she had been before, but inwardly she was torn by a pain that would have no ending because there was no help for it and the wound was too deep for healing.

She had two visitors that afternoon, Alastair Carmichael and Marigold Vibor. Like many men, the editor was uncomfortable in a sickroom and left after being reassured that the damage to her wrist and fingers wouldn't put a permanent end to Carla's photography, but Marigold stayed on for a while.

There was an awkward silence and Carla felt guilty. She knew her listlessness had embarrassed Alastair and now she was probably making Marigold uncomfortable as well, but making polite conversation, difficult at the best of times, required an effort quite beyond her just now.

Marigold said abruptly, 'Look, Carla, I don't want to sound callous, but isn't this intense depression a little abnormal? Or could it be hormonal, sort of like post-natal depression? I mean, you've had a miscarriage, but you're young and there'll be other babies.'

'No.' Carla's voice was flat and lifeless and she avoided her friend's too-astute eyes.

'No?' Marigold's voice had grown thoughtful. 'Why—no? Carla, this Scarlet O'Hara stunt of yours— Revel didn't push you down the stairs, did he?'

'No.'

She could have added drily—Quite the reverse, he thinks I threw myself down. But an odd sort of loyalty to Revel held her silent. She didn't want Marigold to know how unjust and irrational he could be.

Though why she should feel she owed him any loyalty, she didn't know, she reflected bitterly after Marigold had gone. Even more inexplicable was her enduring love for him. His lack of trust, his lack of regard should have killed her feeling for him many times over, but all that happened was that her love became more and more deeply entrenched. It was ineradicable and irrevocable. Even now, in the midst of her own pain and loss, far more lacerating still was the memory of the pain she had glimpsed in Revel's eyes last night—regret for the child he had wanted as much as she had.

In a way, it could be even worse for him than for her, she knew. Men couldn't weep, not men like Revel Braden anyway, and what other emotional outlet did he have, save those wild violent rides down to Chapman's Peak? And believing that she had deliberately destroyed their child would only serve to harden his cynicism and embitter him.

If only she could have made him believe in her, but he was so quick to judge and his understanding of the person she was was so distorted, that it was futile to try—and pointless too, since their marriage was over.

When he arrived that evening, the hatred still burnt in his eyes, shrivelling what small courage she possessed, so that she sat still and silent under his scrutiny, a picture of painful introversion.

Revel's lips twisted in a travesty of a smile after he had examined her pale face and shadowed eyes. 'I'm told you were somewhat . . . upset after I left last night.'

Carla's eyes flickered, her distress palpable. Her lips moved silently as she realised that privacy was impossible in a hospital. Naturally, her state of mind last night had been reported to her husband.

'Yes,' she managed eventually.

'And you're still suffering, aren't you?' he proved insistently.

'Revel. . . .' She looked up to protest, but seeing the implacable contempt darkening his face, it didn't seem worth it. He would never change, his opinion of her would never alter. Revel wanted revenge, and if ever she should betray her love for him, she would be supplying him with the perfect instrument. He would grant her no mercy and she would be destroyed utterly.

Revel lifted a hand, then dropped it again, seeming to change his mind about something.

He said curtly, 'I've asked that you be discharged tomorrow as I have to fly to Beirut the day after. I've telephoned your mother and told her I'll be bringing you to the farm for a few weeks' recuperation, since that is what your own doctor, Basson, advises, and anyway, you won't be able to use your cameras until your wrist and fingers are better. God! Didn't it occur to you that you'd be risking permanent disablement when you hurled yourself down those stairs? Or were you so determined to get rid of my child and make it look like an accident that you were even prepared to sacrifice your career to that end?'

Carla shook her head tiredly, knowing it was futile to argue, and anyway, all her spirit had deserted her. She felt weak, passive, ready to accept anything he handed out, and while she knew it was contemptible of her, she just didn't have the strength to go on fighting.

'My lecturing?' she questioned tonelessly.

'The university has granted you sick leave, but you shouldn't actually miss too much as the winter vacation starts soon.' Revel paused. 'We'll leave as soon as you're discharged tomorrow. Is there anything special you want packed?'

'Anything will do,' Carla supplied apathetically. 'Pasht?'

'Yes, you'll have to take her with you. She has a travelling basket?'

'Yes.' Carla's mind drifted briefly to Pasht, the innocent catalyst of this latest disaster, then skipped to something Revel had said. 'Beirut?'

'Beirut. Poor, bloody Beirut.' The hostility was gone from his eyes as he looked back to another time and place. 'It says everything about its history in recent years to say that my colleagues and I are probably more familiar with Beirut than any other city in the world. . . . The days we've spent skipping from zone to zone, wondering if we'll all still be alive to spend the night fighting over the two telephone lines and four telex machines at the Commodore. . . . Hell, I even rented an apartment there at one stage. It became my home.'

Carla shuddered inwardly. Before she knew him, she had heard it said that Revel Braden had a deathwish and, seeing again the conflict of disgust and a strange devotion that hardened his face when he spoke of his work, she wondered if it was true. Certainly, he was, in a sense, careless of himself, but why? Didn't even loving Vivienne Franck give him enough to live for? She thought of the child they had just lost and wondered if that might have made a difference.

Her almond-shaped eyes were mysteriously downcast, concealing this extra burden of anguish now assailing her. Revel had been cruel to her, never once showing her even a modicum of tenderness, and he had seemed the ultimate in hard self-sufficiency, but now she realised that she saw him as one devil-driven and doomed. A soft silent sigh escaped her. If Vivienne couldn't save him—from himself and the disaster he deliberately courted—then how could she?

She didn't even have the right to try. Their marriage was over. He had swept her ruthlessly into his world of dark, tortured passion, giving her very few choices and robbing her of the will to make independent decisions, but now he was getting rid of her, thrusting her out of his life as brutally as she had drawn her into it. Driving her to the farm was probably the last thing he would ever do for and with her, a swift tidying away of a loose end it disturbed him to see.

Constraint lay heavily on them during the drive north and through the desert the next day. Pasht, protesting in her basket, had more to say than either of them and, noting Revel's impatience when they had to stop and put Pasht on her leash before letting her make use of the sand at the edge of the road, Carla knew he was anxious to be rid of her.

For once in her life she felt no joy in her homecoming, only a sort of relief. Things were cleaner and clearer here in the land of her birth and perhaps some of the dark spectres haunting her might be exorcised.

Revel refused to stay the night at the farm, despite the almost full day's drive they had made, and Carla was torn between fear for him making the long, mind-fazing journey on endless, isolated roads back to Cape Town, when he must be tired after the northward trip, and relief, because her mother, a conventional woman, would have expected them to share a room.

Her parents, brother and sister-in-law, she noted during the couple of hours that Revel took before starting his return journey, were awed by him and treated him with a respect either shy or wary, depending on their character. In return, he was courteous and reserved, refraining from the ironical remarks she had feared, but when his eyes rested on her three-year-old nephew, Carla saw a bleak bitterness in them and knew he was thinking of the child he believed she had destroyed.

In a way, she supposed, their child had been destroyed. They had created it between them and then destroyed it, an innocent victim of their destruction of each other. But now the conflict was at an end, and Carla didn't know if the long solitude ahead of her would be kinder or crueller than their previous tearing apart of each other.

It was the knowledge that she would probably never see Revel again that prompted her to go out to his car with him when the time came for him to leave, her family tactfully remaining in the mellow old farmhouse where generations of the Duminy family had been born.

He ignored her hesitantly murmured thanks and farewell, but didn't get into his car immediately. Instead, he stood staring out into the moonwashed desert with its arid emptiness and the strange shapes of the grotesque succulent plant life which was all that could survive out here.

He said slowly, 'Perhaps I should have seen your desert before involving myself with you. I might have known what to expect. You ... embody the same qualities—farouche and secretive, pitilessly unyielding, it destroys all that is alien to it. . . . As you destroyed our child.'

. 'I didn't——' She had to make one last attempt to free him of his bitterness but that was as far as she got. Revel's arms were fiercely crushing about her as he strained her to him and his mouth ground savagely over hers in an assault that was no farewell salute but a punishment. Then she was turned violently away and she could hear Revel's attempt to steady his harsh, erratic breathing as he got into the car.

Trembling fingertips pressed to her lips, Carla stood and watched him drive away. He had wanted her, she had felt that, and God, he must hate himself for it. But this time he was refusing to let himself sink any deeper into self-disgust. He was getting out of her life.

She started back to the house. Her family looked at her and then looked away, embarrassed, as she hesitated at the lounge door, but it wasn't until she reached her old bedroom that she realised there were tears streaming down her face.

It was a long, bitter night, dark and tormented, with anguish attendant upon her every step as she roamed the infernal regions of misery in those sleepless hours. That night, she touched the depths of the despair that degrades the human spirit by tempting it to give up the struggle for survival and triumph. Once, before she had known Revel, she had dreamed of perfection, of a love that was beauty. Now she felt that if she could not have even the ugly, distorted thing that was the devil's mocking imitation of love, and all that Revel offered her, then she wanted to die.

But Carla came of a line which had survived the desert, never conquering its desolation but learning to endure and even live in uneasy harmony with it and, after learning the truth of the saying that the darkest hour was just before the dawn, she emerged from the crucible with some sort of shaky philosophy. It was better this way, better that Revel had abandoned her. If he had kept her with him, she would eventually have been driven to the ultimate folly of begging for his love.

Yes, it was better so.

The desert couldn't heal her but it did soothe her, its vast emptiness reflecting her own condition. She learned to cope with being alive when all that had made living bearable was dead, her baby, hope and joy. She learned to endure the aching hours of longing for the dark lover and husband who had never been truly a lover but rather a taker, a destroyer, and she learned to be calm and smile again and hide the raw pain of regret behind her automatic good manners.

The fact that the only people she saw in those weeks were her family helped her. As reserved as she, they never touched already throbbing wounds by raising personal subjects. No one asked if she was happy or why she had married such a man as Revel Braden; they would regard such questions as impolite curiosity. Her brother Emil was running the farm these days although her father still worked too and would until the day he died, so Carla's time was spent either alone or with her mother and Linda, but none of the intimate feminine conversations that might have been expected arose. It was not their way, and she wondered if other people would find them strange.

Only Shaun, her small nephew, had the power to distress her as she watched him trotting about at the tasks he performed with earnest self-importance, or trying to restrain his natural exuberance after it was explained to him that Pasht preferred gentle stroking to being manhandled and carried awkwardly about the place. Carla would look at him and remember the way Revel had done so, and she knew she felt exactly what he had felt—they might have had a child like this, even with those same dreaming hazel eyes which ran in the Duminy family. Or with slanting blue-green eyes and a reckless look, she would think sadly.

But she learned to bear such thoughts as well. She was surviving, but that alone took all her strength. She made no decisions or plans and never looked to the future. She was like an ex-addict, taking one day at a time, getting through it, and tomorrow was another battle she would face when it came.

Physically, she mended completely, but weeks passed and she had no thoughts of returning to Cape Town.

Nor did she touch the cameras Revel had included in her luggage, though the emotional mending might have made some progress had she done so. Later on, she supposed, she would have to think about her career, and she expected that Alastair Carmichael would be glad to have her back. She would also have to think about a divorce.

What she didn't anticipate was that Revel would come to fetch her.

She paled, staring as if at a ghost, since she had not expected to see him again, when she returned from an aimless walk one morning and saw him step out of the shade of the verandah and start walking to meet her. His eyes, she saw when he was near enough, were hard, his facial expression tightly controlled.

'Well, Carla, are you ready to come back into the world?' His voice was lightly mocking and his eyes flicked over her without betraying emotion, but lingered on certain feminine curves until she felt colour heating her cheeks while her stomach tightened. 'Alastair Carmichael wants you to fly to Zambia next week to get some photos for an article on mining up there. Can you be packed and ready to leave after lunch—which your mother is preparing at the moment?'

'Yes,' she responded automatically, still shocked by his arrival. 'I . . . I wasn't expecting you to come and fetch me.'

'It makes sense since your own car is still sitting in Cape Town,' Revel pointed out laconically.

Caught off balance by his arrival, Carla was too disturbed to make much protest, but at least the knowledge of the assignment to Zambia had restored one thing to her, her professional pride. Without conceit, she knew no one could do mining photos as originally as she. She packed and, after lunch, said a reserved goodbye to her family, looking back at them as they drove away with a faint sense of loss, a feeling that the gulf between them would grow wider and wider as time went by.

They belonged to the desert still, but she had made the transition. She was going back to the city, where she belonged—and to that end, she could endure being with Revel for a few hours. Her mind began to clear and a thought struck her——

'Where will I . . . I suppose I can stay with Marigold or go to a hotel until I find another flat,' she speculated quietly.

There was a short silence during which she became aware of a mounting tension.

Then Revel said silkily, 'No, Carla, you're coming home with me. You are my wife, and you will share my house and my bed.'

CHAPTER TEN

'REVEL, please won't you let me go?' Carla appealed once more, soon after her return from Zambia. Her voice was quietly composed, but her hands were tense as they toyed with her small fruit knife.

They had just eaten dinner and were lingering at the table while the coffee was percolating. It was almost two weeks since he had fetched her from the Karoo, and Carla had been protesting ever since—and yet not protesting as much as she could have done, she realised with a feeling of shame. She didn't have to stay here with him; she could have walked out, but she hadn't. But now it was becoming too much to bear again, and she knew she couldn't take much more. It was all happening as it had before. They lived in the same house, saw each other occasionally, and shared a bed, yet Revel rarely came to that bed until two or three in the morning. Once again, he was going out in the evenings, sometimes without an explanation, sometimes claiming he had reports to compile for his overseas broadcasting clients, and Carla guessed that he was still seeing Vivienne Franck.

He had to be, because he never touched her. Revel was a passionately sensual man, accustomed to having his physical needs assuaged, and if Vivienne hadn't been satisfying him, surely he would have turned to his wife, however much he hated her and despised himself. But if he had Vivienne, why was he so insistent that she stay with him? Carla shivered as the only possible answer came to her, and not for the first time. Revenge ... punishment! She constantly endeavoured to conceal her gnawing unhappiness behind a façade of conventional courtesy, but occasionally it would burst out, too overwhelmingly intense to be contained, and then she would see the cruel glint in his blue-green eyes and know that he was congratulating himself.

'You know my answer, Carla,' Revel stated now.

'But ... Revel, for pity's sake, I can't take much more of this!' Carla was surprised at the way the anguished words came flooding out of her. She had not intended to admit that and let him know just how successfully he was torturing her with the situation he had deliberately created. She bowed her shame-stricken head and added in a stifled voice, 'What's the point of going on? There's no reason for us to stay married. ... The reason doesn't exist any more.'

'You made sure of that, didn't you?' Revel accused savagely. 'But otherwise you're wrong. Just because I never touch you, it doesn't mean I don't want you. I do. ... Haven't you realised yet that you're an obsession with me, damn you? Do you think I enjoy it. ... Admitting that for the first time in my life there is something I can't control? I despise myself, but I can't help it. ... The devil knows why.'

His bitter admission shocked her, as well as shaming her. She said swiftly and breathlessly, 'Then give me my freedom, Revel, please! Then you wouldn't see me. ... You wouldn't have to despise yourself!'

'I can't! I can't let you go, Carla.' Revel's face was dark and drawn as he pushed back his chair and stood up. 'I have to go out this evening, so I'll skip the coffee, but let me warn you now—*I* can't take much more of this. Soon now I shall expect you to commit yourself to a normal relationship.'

'Do you mean—sex?' Carla asked candidly, her emotions so turbulent they overruled shyness.

'What else?'

'And you call that a normal relationship?' she condemned scathingly, getting to her feet. 'Sex without love isn't normal, and humiliating me by forcing me to beg.... That's not normal either, Revel, but that's the way it will be, won't it?'

'If you resume that stupid pretence of not wanting me,' he confirmed, pausing at the door. 'Because in that, at least, you've sunk as low as I have, Carla.'

She saw the glitter of a dark, bitter hunger in his eyes and felt an answering surge of hot sweet desire in her loins before shame overtook her. Nothing was changed. Still it was only her body that obsessed him. Other than that, he felt nothing but hatred and contempt, and to yield even once more to those would be to abandon self-respect for ever.

'Hasn't it occurred to you that your treatment of me might have killed whatever desire I once felt for you?' she ventured stiffly, knowing it was untrue. She would always love him, she would always want him——

'We'll see,' Revel was saying coolly. 'And soon, Carla, very soon.'

Then he was gone and she found she was gripping the back of her chair so tightly that her knuckles showed white through the tautly stretched skin. She was trembling violently with distress, her thoughts and emotions in turmoil.

Dear God, what was she to do? Sanity dictated that she make her escape now, while she was still free to do so. If Revel took her again, she would be entering an eternity of intolerable bondage, and her mind might follow her pride to its sordid grave. She would become more and more enslaved, a despised chattel, a passive toy just waiting for the times when his sadistic streak demanded entertainment and brought her to life, spiritless and humiliated in between those times.

And yet she could not go. Was she really stupid enough to imagine that their marriage had any chance at all, with all that lay between them and behind them, the bitterness, the suspicion and the hatred? Revel's desire for her was a dark, driving compulsion, terrifying in its intensity, but she was a fool if she hoped it could measure up to his towering love for Vivienne Franck. Love was the invincible, shining citadel that endured and triumphed, lust merely a dark, erotic abyss from which he must eventually haul himself because a man like Revel Braden couldn't go on despising himself forever. He had too much pride.

The following day was Friday and Carla was still no nearer a decision by the time she returned from a late afternoon meeting at the university. She garaged her car, noticing that Revel must be at home as the Lamborghini was parked in the driveway, indicating that he intended going out again. She sighed. That was nothing new.

He met her in the hall and Carla experienced the return of an old fear on seeing that he was carrying an overnight bag.

'You . . . you're going away?' she questioned stiltedly, afraid of revealing herself.

'We're both going away—to the cottage for the weekend,' Revel informed her with a mocking smile. 'You've got five minutes. I've packed for you—not that you'll be needing much—and Ramira has agreed to look after Pasht.'

She was too inhibited to retaliate with threats of screaming and making a scene, and she bowed her head in defeat, hating herself for being the way she was. If she was being executed, she would probaby feel obliged to thank her executioner politely when he blindfolded her.

'You see, Carla,' Revel explained with what sounded like deceptive mildness when they were in his car and speeding towards the Point. 'I can't wait any longer. It's time you were a real wife to me again, and where better to make this second beginning than at the cottage, with its memories, and where we'll be able to concentrate exclusively on each other?'

He sounded so casual but, sensitive to every nuance of his voice, Carla caught the underlying note of steely intent. She shivered, though she wasn't cold. She was wearing a casually elegant palest orchid velour jumpsuit and it had been one of those rare days, at the end of a long cold winter, that held out hope of a coming spring.

Revel meant to have her, she knew, and there could be no escape. He had only to touch her. . . . On one thing she was resolved. She would offer no resistance, She would endure this weekend, but unless she could make Revel listen to her and believe that Vivienne had lied to him on the night of her fall, she would leave him. Already she bore too many scars.

Ramira Maglas had packed a large container of provisions and on arrival at the cottage, Carla cooked a light supper. She kept remembering the first time Revel had brought her here, her nervousness then. Tonight, though, she had passed beyond fear, accepting her lot fatalistically except for the quick excitement that licked through her veins whenever she anticipated the union to come. She supposed she was being self-indulgent, snatching this one last time for herself, to keep and cherish in the time when memories were all she would have left, and none of those memories wholly sweet, each one tinged with bitterness.

This time they both had wine with their meal, and coffee in the comfortable lounge afterwards. It was colder down here close to the Point than it had been in Cape Town, and the wind, a sighing murmur while they ate, now rose in pitch to a wild shriek. Carla looked up and found Revel's eyes on her, broodingly cynical, and she moistened her lips, an unconsciously provocative gesture. Now might be the time to appeal to him, to get him to listen to her and believe that she had not deliberately destroyed their child She could offer him another child, if only he would believe her.

'Revel,' she began softly, palms turned outward in a pacific gesture. 'Revel, can we talk? Will you listen to me and——'

'Later!' He was on his feet, coming towards her, and she saw that a mask had fallen from his face, leaving his blatant hunger naked for her to see. 'I've waited long enough for you, Carla, weeks and endless weeks of waiting, aching to feel your body shuddering and responsive beneath mine, to know again your warmth about me . . . I won't wait any longer. I want you now!'

She was hauled roughly to her feet and pulled against the hard length of his body, feeling its heat through the thin silk of his slate-blue shirt. Mindful of her resolve not to protest, she said as calmly as she could, 'Can't I . . . bath, first?'

'No!'

His mouth swooped to savage hers, but eventually he drew back.

'God! How do you do this to me, Carla? Why you? Out of all the women in the world. . . .' His eyes glittered with disgust as he stared at her. 'Damn you! Touch me, look at me, and see the effect you have on me.'

Carla's eyes strayed irresistibly downwards and deep colour stained her cheeks as she witnessed the evidence of his arousal. Then she looked at his tortured face and was overwhelmed by a surging rush of love for him.

'Revel.' Sighing her surrender, she drew him back to her.

She was naked when he lifted her and carried her to the bedroom, and his pounding desire was matched by hers. It had never been this way before, she realised as she writhed erotically beneath a hundred burning kisses and caresses, never this dark, never so intense. The rage to possess her made Revel savage, a little hurtful, but she didn't heed the pain because she too was touched by that madness exulting in the groaning response her seductively straying hands and lips drew from him, their mingled perspiration soaking their bodies, making them glisten bronze and ivory in the small light that poured its soft radiance over them.

They were white-hot flame in each other's arms, searing, consuming each other. It was immolation, ecstasy and death by fire, as they hurtled towards the moment when they must become one. Their bodies must join, but the two separate, tortured spirits that had never yet met still stood aside, watching appalled at the devouring, destructive passion that knew nothing of tenderness or consideration.

Bitter, raggedly disjointed words tore from Revel's throat. 'Why you, Carla? And why . . . me?' It was an agonised question to which she had no answer, aroused beyond endurance by the closeness of their bodies that still weren't close enough.

'Why are you waiting?' she moaned, clinging convulsively, her slender body racked by long tremors.

'What do you want, Carla?'

A silent scream filled her mind and she felt herself toppling into a hot black abyss, hating him but still wanting him, more than she had ever done before.

'Oh, God, no! You said if I was honest you wouldn't do this, Revel,' she gasped painfully, twisting and turning with frustration as he denied her the final rapture she craved. 'And I have been honest, I haven't denied that . . . I . . . want you.'

'But there's still so much that you withhold from me,' he grated, his eyes ablaze with some daemonic emotion as they slid over her white face. 'So I'll have your pleas instead.'

On the brink of ecstasy, she knew she could not turn back. 'All right, I am begging you, please. . . .'

Her own voice sobbing that last word over and over

again was a nightmare of humiliation, but not until she felt her thighs nudged apart did her voice die, and then the only sound was her bitter weeping as he took her. Tears poured from her and she knew she was crying for him as well as herself.

But even weeping, she whirled and soared with him through the spiralling crimson darkness until together they broke the chains of their mortality and had their brief time in the piercing white light of true and complete ecstasy.

To return, to fall back to earth . . . Carla heard the shrieking daemons' mockery and felt their hands clutching her, dragging her down once more, and the pain of it was almost physical.

'You bastard, Revel.' Her forlorn whisper contained despair, and perhaps Revel's answering groan as he turned away from her meant that he too found the descent intolerable.

She waited only until her breathing had slowed and her limbs ceased from trembling. Then she left the bed, uncaring whether Revel had fallen asleep or not. She found her old golden velour robe that he had packed for her—she had never worn the garnet one again since the night she had fallen downstairs and lost their baby.

Tying the girdle about her waist with clumsy fingers, she made for the door. She had to get away, to be alone, and think——

'Where are you going, Carla?'

'Out! Anywhere?' She cast a wild glance back at him. 'Away from you!'

'Wait!'

She fled, running blindly through the cottage and outside, too distracted by grief to know what she did. She didn't care, she didn't think, she only knew that what had just occurred must never be allowed to happen again.

'Carla!'

She turned and saw that he was coming after her, having stopped only to don jeans.

'No!' She was barefoot, but she didn't stop when she found herself at the top of the low cliffs though she hardly knew how she came to be there. Jagged stones cut her feet, and low sea shrubs caught at her robe, but she ran on, slithering over the short uneven steps cut into the lower part of the path, heedless of everything save the need to get away from her tormentor.

She was utterly, unreasoningly panic-stricken, and consequently unthinking, her flight as wild and instinctive as that of a small animal fleeing a predator, but Revel was swifter than she and caught up with her on the beach where the howling wind lifted stinging grains of sand and tore the sound from their mouths.

'Carla, for God's sake, what are you doing? Come back to the cottage with me——'

'No, not again, I can't bear it,' she cried frantically. 'Never again, Revel, never!'

His hands were reaching for her but she turned and ran from him. She was in the dark, and the icy sea was swirling about her ankles and weighting the hem of her robe. Its wild, furious sound, as the wind tossed waves violently in every direction, filled her ears and her mind, and the icy water numbed her flesh and froze her bones, paralysing her. A larger wave caught her about the thighs, throwing her to her knees, and she was unable to stand up again, her robe heavy and soaked with water, but strong arms were about her.

'No!' Still she struggled, desperate to escape him.

'For God's sake, Carla, do you want to drown?' Revel's voice was taut and urgent.

'Yes! I'd rather be dead than be humiliated by you like that again.'

'You won't be, I can promise you that,' Revel's harsh voice reached her. 'I'll never touch you again after I've got you out of here, I swear.'

Sanity returned like a blow. Appalled by what she had done and shamed by her hysterical display, Carla collapsed against him as he raised her, and she mumbled stupidly, 'Feet . . . cramp.'

She was only half-conscious and recalled little of how he carried her out of the sea and up to the cottage, and it was only later when he had helped her into a warm bath and then dried her and dressed her once more in the velour jumpsuit that full awareness returned.

'You win, Carla,' Revel said wearily, watching her sip the brandy he had given her and then passing her a mug of tea. 'Drink that and we'll go back to Cape Town.'

She had never known him sound and look so bleak. The flesh seemed to have been stripped from his face, leaving the bones starkly prominent, with dark shadows beneath them, and she knew an urge to reach out, to comfort and be comforted, but she lacked the courage to make such a gesture now, when only rejection lay in the sea-coloured eyes.

She said gently, 'I don't really want to die, you know.'

'Not now, and not before,' he agreed heavily. 'But I think you meant it at the moment of saying it.'

'I was hysterical,' Carla began reassuringly, but he had turned away and she was left feeling guilty— because her stupid action had added to whatever burden of guilt he bore.

It was still dark when they returned to Cape Town, and Revel said curtly, 'Go to bed and get some sleep, Carla. I'll use one of the other bedrooms. I may have to go out in the morning, but I'll wait until Ramira arrives.'

He wasn't going to leave her alone in the house, Carla realised sadly. He didn't trust her. . . .

An excess of emotion and the struggle in the sea had exhausted her. She slept soundly until ten o'clock and woke to find Revel gone and Ramira Malgas busy in the downstairs rooms.

'Mr Braden said will you stay around until he gets back?' Ramira passed on the message while Carla made coffee. 'He expects to have news for you.'

What sort of news? Carla's thoughts were sad and grey, in contrast to the day which was clear and almost windless, wrapped in the tender warmth of a pale sun. Later she made more coffee and took it outside, seating herself on the stone wall beside one of the sunken paths, accompanied by Pasht who soon deserted her in order to explore the garden. It was one of Basheer Malgas's days and he was at the far end of the driveway, oiling the big wooden gates.

Carla watched him absently as strange, sad little thoughts drifted through her mind and were allowed to disperse, because it was too much effort to cling to them. Her body felt stiff and sore, a result, she supposed, of last night's tempestuous lovemaking followed by her fight in the sea, but her heart was even more bruised. It was a dreary, leaden weight in her breast, and a tight knot of unhappiness was constricting her throat. She knew she ought to be thinking, planning, but she seemed incapable of doing so, weak and helpless. Wryly she wondered if she was suffering some sort of emotional breakdown, with last night's insane action the first stage.

It was twelve o'clock when the Lamborghini purred up the driveway, causing Pasht to streak for the safety of the house, and Carla lifted her head as Revel got out and walked slowly towards her. He looked as drained and weary as she felt, she reflected, seeing the shadowy look about his eyes and the way he was keeping his mouth tightly compressed.

He stopped in front of her and Carla tensed on seeing the stormy expression in his eyes as they roamed over her, noting her outfit of pale apricot pleated pants, loose in the leg but tight about her slender ankles and narrow waist, worn with a loose matching crossover top. She had washed her hair and it shone in the sun, a rich satiny brown, reaching to her shoulders these days and curling inward. Her face was innocent of make-up though, and she felt suddenly naked, meeting his look with wary defensiveness.

'You can stop looking like that, Carla,' he advised tautly. 'You're free. Leave whenever you want—but don't feel obligated to hurry it. If you need time to make arrangements, I'll use one of the spare bedrooms. I'll speak to a lawyer on Monday. All right?'

Her head was bent as she murmured, 'Yes. Thank you.'

When she looked up, he had gone inside. A sigh shuddered through her slender frame. There had been no need to make a decision. Revel had done it for her, and she could guess why. Her mad action last night had shaken him; he didn't want the responsibility, should she do something similar again. Carla was sorry about that, knowing him well enough to be aware that deep within him, probably not even admitted to himself, guilt would be tearing at him. But at least her brief insanity had achieved this end and she didn't have to fight for her freedom. She couldn't have gone on living with him. She might have endured and forgiven anything—except his lack of love.

Carla spent another night in the house, alone in the double bed. Unable to face a hotel and with Pasht to consider, she knew Marigold Vibor would welcome her until she found another flat, although she guessed she would never get anything as ideal as the old one. The trouble was, she had been unable to contact Marigold, finally learning from someone at the *Afrinews* offices that she would only be back from Mozambique the following morning.

Strangely, Revel had remained at home after telling her she was free, and he didn't even go out in the evening. Carla lay in bed, knowing he was downstairs in the lounge, and once she crept to the head of the stairs and heard the clink of glass on glass. He was drinking, and earlier this evening he had started smoking again, something he rarely did. She stayed awake for some hours after that, afraid that if he got drunk, he would forget his promise that she was free, but he still hadn't come upstairs when, eventually, she dropped into a troubled sleep.

A Sunday morning silence hung over the house when she got up, dressing in jeans and a blue shirt, and neither she nor Revel did anything to disturb it, avoiding being in the same room together, unspeaking when they encountered each other. They had nothing left to say.

Carla telphoned Marigold and got her permission to stay with her for a few days.

'I'll come when I've packed,' she concluded, knowing she would face an interrogation when she got there.

She started packing immediately and there were clothes and photographic equipment strewn about the room when Revel knocked at the open door. He was wearing black and looked tired, but his eyes were guarded.

'Yes?' Her own eyes were wide, her voice husky from disuse.

'I'd like to know what you've arranged ... where you're going?'

'I'm staying with Marigold until I find another flat,' Carla supplied tonelessly. 'I. ... The furniture I brought here. Can I leave it for the time being?'

'Of course.' His dark face was resolutely controlled, his eyes inscrutable as he came further into the room, looking over her belongings without expression. He picked up her portfolio of private photos from the bed, almost absently, and began to look through it. Carla

gazed at him uncertainly for a few seconds, then
resumed packing. Her pulses leapt nervously when he
spoke again. 'You can photograph humanity, after all.'
He put down the portfolio and smiled grimly at her. 'I
used to accuse you of cowardice, but it's really a surfeit
of compassion, isn't it?'

'I suppose it's cowardice in a way,' she allowed
carefully, disconcerted by his choice of subject at such a
time. 'Not being able to face other people's . . . pain.'

'Sensitivity,' he mused quietly. 'I think I always
sensed that in you. You were so far above me there, I
couldn't hope to match you. I suppose that's why I was
always taunting you, calling it cowardice.'

'It doesn't matter,' Carla said flatly.

'No, nothing matters any more.' Revel suddenly
sounded infinitely weary. He walked to the window and
stared out at the mountain, so close, because
Rondebosch lay in its shadow but Carla knew he wasn't
seeing it. She went to the dressing-table and began to
lift bottles of scent distractedly, but stopped when he
resumed tiredly, 'Carla, I want to tell you. . . . You have
the right to know that I am . . . aware of how cruelly I
have misjudged you and consequently abused you. I
went to see Bernard Franck yesterday morning. You
were so unhappy—I wanted to ask him if he could give
you any sort of future. . . . He told me you weren't in
love with him, that there had never been anything
between you. Oh, he loves you, but I don't think he
would ever have tried to take it further. You're the
romantic ideal he worships from afar, his perfect
woman, the total opposite of Vivienne. He also told me
the truth about a number of things; your friendship
with him, why he had been at your flat that night I first
made love to you. . . . That you'd seen his daughter at
some foul religious rally and he had wanted to talk
about it. . . . And he told me why he was here the night
you lost the baby, that you'd been trying to find me,

and about the cat frightening you. . . . God, Carla! You wanted the baby, didn't you?'

'Yes,' she confirmed curtly. It was still too painful to be discussed. She stared at him straight back, seeing the terrible tension in his shoulders and the slightly inclined angle of his dark head. Was this why he seemed so—at a loss? Because Bernard had assured him that there was no chance of his freeing Vivienne? 'Revel. . . .'

'Oh, God!' The violent words seemed torn from him and he sounded as if he were in pain, but still he kept his back to her. 'I'm sorry, I am so sorry, though I know there's no sort of apology I can make for the terrible damage I've done, and nothing that will mend it. I'm just no good to you, I never have been, but I wish, I wish, I'd handled it all differently. I wish I hadn't made you hate me.'

'I don't hate you,' Carla whispered, shocked to hear him so unusually humble.

'No, you're too kind to hate anyone, but hatred is all I deserve.' Now his voice was dead, flat and somehow resigned. 'I wish you weren't going . . . I love you so much and I've broken you, and God knows, it's killing me. I've been existing in a sort of hell since the first time I saw you, though I tried to pretend I didn't love you, that you weren't worth it, for my own protection as much as anything.

'I thought you were having an affair with Bernard Franck—I think Vivienne first put the idea in my mind when she realised I liked to hear her talk about you. She had been trying to inititate an affair between us for years and suddenly she had found a way of holding my interest, by complaining that you were having an affair with Bernard. I was so desperate to hear any small thing about you, that even hearing that, over and over again, was preferable to nothing. . . .

'Eventually it got so bad, I couldn't fight it any longer, and I had to force my way into your life. I told

myself I could take you away from Franck ... I
suppose I was making excuses to myself for the way I
was ... persecuting you, when you clearly hated me. I
pretended I was doing the Francks a favour, but that
night I took you to the restaurant in Sea Point,
knowing they'd be there, I was doing it purely for my
own benefit. I wanted you, but I'll admit that I did
hope that Vivienne's obsession would die a natural
death if she could see for herself that I was truly
committed, that I loved you, because she knew me well
enough to see that my feeling for you was more,
something real, compared to the transitory interest I
had had in women like Noelle Malherbe, who never
deterred Vivienne's pursuit. That part of it didn't work
either because, as I see now, she was determined to get
rid of you. She lost no opportunity of reiterating that
you and Bernard were in love and, God forgive me, I
believed her. I'd known her most of my life and ... oh,
hell!

'Eventually she turned up at my Johannesburg hotel
when I was there covering the last Soweto riots and to
get rid of her once and for all, I told her straight out
how much I loved you and how much I wanted our
child—thereby giving her yet another weapon to use
against you when you fell down those stairs. The risk
she took, though. ... If she'd been there when I saw
Franck yesterday, I'd have killed her. But, my God,
Carla, I'll never forgive myself for that night. I
frightened you, didn't I? You never had a chance to
defend yourself.'

Carla was trembling uncontrollably, still hardly able
to take in what she was hearing. She stared at his back
and saw how tightly he was gripping the windowsill,
while his head was bent even lower than before.

She said the first thing that came into her head:
'Revel, all those nights you went out and left me alone
... I thought you were with Vivienne. She lied to me

about things too. . . . If you loved me, why did you stop making love to me, and where were you all those nights?'

He made a sound that was supposed to be a laugh and her heart contracted painfully. 'I was keeping away from temptation. I couldn't take your hatred any more, the resentment you always showed after I'd made love to you, and I knew if I stayed in the house I wouldn't be able to control myself. I've never had any control where you were concerned. Carla. I was so jealous of Franck and so resentful of the fact that you didn't love me, and I used to take my anger out on you, punishing you for not loving me. I knew I could make you want me, though, and that's why I used to make you beg like that, God help me. I was like a miser, gloating over your desire, treasuring it, because I couldn't have your love.'

He paused, standing absolutely motionless, before asking in a raw, self-deriding tone, 'Carla, I need to know, although either answer will put me in hell for the rest of my life—if I had handled things differently, could I have made you love me, or was there never any chance?'

Carla took a hesitant step towards him, then stopped, her eyes brimming with tears as she raised trembling fingers to her mouth. They had both been tortured long enough and she had to get the words right this time, and not let shyness prevent complete understanding.

'I did love you, Revel.' Her voice cracked with an intolerable mixture of joy and anguish and regret. 'How, if I didn't love you, could I have let you make love to me that first time? You . . . you needed me, and I wanted to give you . . . I had just realised that I did and——'

Revel had swung round, his eyes mirroring the incredulity she was feeling, but then his shoulders slumped and he turned back to the window. 'I note your consistent use of the past tense, Carla, and it's not more than I deserve, though God knows how I'm going to exist without you.'

'I always use the wrong words, don't I?' Carla drew a shaking breath. 'I still love you, Revel.'

He stiffened. 'Is this pity, Carla?' he questioned jerkily. 'That compassion you possess in such abundance?'

'Disbelieving to the end,' she murmured wryly as she reached him, laying a hand on his shoulder and feeling him flinch. He turned, his face pale as he searched her expression. 'You've never trusted me before. . . . Couldn't you begin now? We've wasted so much.'

'And I've destroyed so much.' Oddly, Revel hesitated, then lifted a hand to her face, a desperate hope flaring in his eyes. 'Is this true, Carla?'

'Does it seem so impossible? Well, perhaps it does, because knowing you love me is like . . . like having a miracle happen. Oh, Revel!' Carla's voice was suddenly choked with emotion and she slid her arms round him and clung, trembling. 'Have you been as unhappy as I have? I loved you so much, and I never dreamed——'

'Ah, God! How can you be generous enough to forgive what I've done?' Revel closed his eyes briefly, then inhaled a shuddering breath. 'I'm at a loss, my darling, a complete loss. How can I tell you, show you——'

Carla lifted her hand to touch his beloved dark face, its harshness strangely softened by the emotion that made him inarticulate. She could feel him shaking and knew that the miracle really had happened.

'You could start with a kiss,' she whispered, stroking his cheek.

Their mouths met, tentatively at first, and then more surely, in a kiss that was apology and forgiveness and finally commitment, a promise for the future, and the greatest miracle of all was in the way Revel touched her and held her, gently, almost reverently, his hands incredibly tender in the way they caressed her body, stroked her hair and touched her face. It was their first kiss of tenderness and Carla felt the sting of tears in her eyes, more moved than she had ever been in her life.

They drew apart a little and Revel's eyes searched her face, as if he still doubted. 'Can we really make it work, this time? With so much bitterness behind us, and all the suffering I've inflicted on you?'

Carla's eyes were very clear as she answered him seriously. 'We have to make it work. We will! We might remember the unhappiness, but it won't colour the happiness we'll make together. Oh, we deserve to be happy after all we've both been through, don't you think?'

She was smiling at him in a way he had never seen before, radiant and confident, and slowly he smiled back, relaxing at last. They were looking into each other's eyes and hearts, and in that moment their spirits saw each other at last and met in the embrace of perfect understanding that makes a true marriage.

'You're wonderful,' Revel said with a shaky laugh, drawing her close again. 'So when do we start making it work?'

Carla's pulses raced as she felt his escalating need of her. 'Like now?' she ventured mischievously, gently freeing herself and going to the bed where she removed the open suitcase, her portfolio and several garments, simply dropping them on the floor.

She turned back to him, drawing a quick shaken breath as she saw his face, and then he came to her.

'Do you know, I'm almost scared?' Revel confessed long rapturous minutes later when nothing was between them.

'Me too.' She laughed, flushed and tremulous. 'It's as if . . . this is the first time, isn't it?'

'It is the first time, the first time we've known. . . .'

It was shatteringly new. When the ache loving desire imposed on their loins became intolerable, they merged wordlessly, and it was a complete merging, a blending of hearts and bodies, minds and spirits, in unutterable delight, a perfect whole at last, and at the end Carla heard Revel gasp words she had dreamed of, while she cried aloud her own love and rapture.

Afterwards she looked down at the dark head resting sweetly heavy against her breasts and lifted a hand to touch it. She didn't think she had tamed him, but she knew he had found peace at last, as she had, and it was enough. This was the first time she had been utterly content in the aftermath of passion, with the sound of Revel's muttered, extravagant endearments still in her ears. This time there was no humiliation. Humility, yes, because she was still awed by a love that matched hers, but pride too, and most of all, the matchless joy of knowing she was loved as well as desired.

After a while, Revel stirred, moving until he was lying beside her, and Carla thought she had never seen his eyes so clear, nothing concealed from her any longer and all bitterness gone.

'I can still hardly believe you love me,' he murmured huskily. 'I wish I had known.'

'I wish I had known about you,' she retorted gently. 'But I thought you'd guess about me when you came home one evening and heard Vivienne saying she had the man I wanted.'

A shadow crossed his face. 'I thought she meant Bernard—especially as, in no sense, did she . . . have me,' Revel added distastefully. A sighing laugh escaped him. 'And I all but told you I loved you then when I said you had what she wanted.'

'I thought you resented being married, that you felt trapped.' There was a little break in Carla's voice and a spasm of pain tightened Revel's face momentarily.

'I only resented the fact that you didn't seem to love me at all, darling,' he told her. 'I wanted you and our child.'

'There'll be another baby, Revel,' she said softly.

'Yes.' His sensitive fingertips traced the line of her cheek and she felt herself melting with love. 'Thank you.'

Carla stretched luxuriously before folding her slim arms about him, laughing a little. 'Oh, I love you so much, I want to promise you everything—the world!'

'I have the world right here beside me.' The unguarded look in his eyes made the breath catch in her throat. 'And it's I who should be making promises to you. You're incredible and I'll give anything, do anything.'

'Just one thing.' Carla hesitated, a little afraid of testing her power, and Revel smiled.

'Yes?'

'Those mad rides of yours. They terrify me.'

'I won't need those any more.' He paused. 'I thought you were going to mention my work.'

'Oh, no. I can't pretend I won't be afraid, that I won't miss you, and hate your absences but ... a man and his work! I'd never ask that of you, Revel,' she murmured.

'Nevertheless, I don't think it'll be for much longer. I've been offered several editorial posts.' Revel looked rueful. 'But I can't pretend it's for your peace of mind as much as for my own selfish sake. I don't want to be parted from you, and suddenly the risks of war reporting don't seem worthwhile.... My life has become too precious, with you in it.'

Cara smiled at him, robbed of words by the privilege of knowing she was responsible for this new contented, deeply caring aspect of his darkly complex and volatile nature.

Then she managed the simple words she knew would

be her creed in their life together. 'If you're happy, so am I.'

'Ah, my dear love.' Revel was moved and showed it. 'You're so ... I love you and need you so much. ... And you?'

'Oh, yes.' Carla could tease now, shyness gone forever in the security he had given her, the knowledge that she was cherished. 'Don't you know yet?'

'I'm beginning to learn.' Revel laughed shakily as his arm tightened about her and he felt the unmistakable response of her slender body. 'It's said there's no such thing as a perfect marriage, that every marriage has its good times and its bad. We've had our bad time, haven't we, Carla? Please God, there's only good ahead of us.'

'The good has already begun,' Carla murmured, offering him her lips and feeling her heart swell with happiness because the old restlessness was gone from her husband's eyes.

The good, the pleasure, and the peace, had begun at last, after their long conflict, and they both knew it would endure, doubly precious for being so dearly bought. Love had defeated bitterness and suspicion, bringing wisdom and trust in their place—love, the only victor.

4
FREE
Harlequin Romances